WICKED PRINCE

A SECRET BABY ROMANCE

LILIAN MONROE

WANT THREE BOOKS DELIVERED STRAIGHT TO YOUR INBOX? HOW ABOUT THREE ROCK STAR ROMANCES THAT WERE *WAY* TOO HOT TO SELL?

GET THE COMPLETE *ROCK HARD* SERIES:
WWW.LILIANMONROE.COM/ROCKHARD

~

1

MARGOT

ATONEMENT.

That's what I'm doing when I haul another tray of baked goods into a cooling rack at my sister's bakery. I move to sweep flour off the floor and smile as my sister comes through the door.

"You don't have to do this, Margot," Ivy says. "I have enough employees. You should just relax."

My sister's black hair is pulled into a sleek ponytail. She wipes her hands on her apron, glancing through the front door of the bakery. Chewing her bottom lip, Ivy wrings her hands. "You think people will come back?"

"It's your grand re-opening," I smile. "Of course they'll come back."

"Even after people were hospitalized because of me?"

"It wasn't because of you," I answer, leaning the broom against the wall. I put my hands on my sister's shoulders. "It was my dickhead agent, Hunter. You were a victim of his maliciousness."

"I know, but you know what I mean. People will still

blame me. Hunter hasn't been charged with anything—besides his confession to you, there's no evidence that he was even here."

I smile. "It'll be fine. Word has gotten out that he planted the bacteria. I've been looking at the response online, and it doesn't look like people blame you at all. All kinds of shady stuff Hunter's done is surfacing, now. If anything, the extra publicity will be good."

"Not for the people who were hospitalized." Ivy grimaces, and my chest squeezes.

I try to swallow past the lump that's lodged itself in my throat. "I'm sorry, Ivy."

Her eyes turn back to me, and she shakes her head. "You know it wasn't your fault."

"If I'd been more supportive..."

"You had just gotten home. You're in recovery. You were taking care of yourself after supporting me your entire life. None of this is your fault." Ivy wraps her arms around me, and my chest tightens some more.

Guilt is a useless emotion. It doesn't serve any purpose. It doesn't push me to be a better person, it only drags me down further into my own anxiety. Feeling guilty doesn't change the past.

Logically, I know this, but the guilt persists.

It snakes in and out of my heart, creeping into my thoughts whenever I feel like I'm doing well. Guilt is a group of little gremlins, hiding in every corner of my mind. They poke their heads out once in a while to remind me that I'm a terrible person.

Even when I spend a week helping Ivy out at her bakery, *Spoonful of Sugar*, and endorse her publicly when she announces that she'll re-open it, I still feel bad.

It was *my* agent who poisoned her food. It was my agent who put her in the hospital. It was my agent who tried to ruin her new business.

Guilty, guilty, guilty.

The back door of the bakery bursts open, and Ivy's boyfriend, Prince Luca, comes through. He gives me a broad smile, hooking his arms around both Ivy and me.

"Today's the big day!"

Ivy's face breaks into a grin, and she nuzzles her face into his chest. The Prince kisses the top of her head.

My heart melts. There was a time when I was jealous of Ivy. It wasn't long ago, either—only about four months. They were the darkest days of my life, right before I learned the truth about my diagnosis. Before I hit rock bottom. I saw the relationship budding between the two of them, and I thought it should be me that Prince Luca wanted, not my sister.

I was in a haze of self-medication, depression, and anxiety. My mind was a mess, and it landed me pregnant, overdosing in hospital, and forced to retreat to an intensive therapy course in the middle of the Farcliff wilderness. I was unhealthy, selfish, and wrong.

I know that now, but it doesn't make it any easier.

I reach for my bottle of water on the counter, and my hand shakes slightly. I look at the tremor in my hand, and fear pierces through me like an ice pick. I ball my hand into a fist to hide the shaking. Glancing at Ivy, I breathe a sigh of relief when I see she hasn't noticed.

I reach for the bottle again, knocking it to the ground.

"Shit," I say under my breath.

Ivy laughs, shaking her head. "Always the clumsy one. How your publicist manages to hide that from the public is beyond me."

"She's a magician," I say, laughing nervously as I pick up the water bottle with trembling hands. "Being an oaf doesn't exactly fit with the image of a 'graceful blonde goddess.'" I grin, making air quotes around the last words.

Ivy giggles. I turn away from her, using a precious moment to take a deep breath and compose myself.

Four months ago—on the same day I somehow overdosed from laced heroin, which I don't remember at all—I tested positive for Huntington's disease. It's the illness that killed our mother.

Ivy and I watched her degenerate slowly over the last twenty years of her life, her brain slowly falling apart from the mutated proteins the disease pumped into her grey matter. She died of pneumonia, which ravaged her weakened immune system, but not before her whole personality transformed into something negative, angry, and sometimes violent.

That's the fate that is awaiting me, too—and no one knows, except me.

Ivy doesn't know about the diagnosis, but she does know about my pregnancy. She thinks I'm just a regular old messed-up celebrity. She thinks life will continue as it has been, and we'll all live happily ever after. She's excited that her child will have a cousin to play with.

I'm trying to think like her. I go to therapy twice a week and I'm taking care of my body with yoga and weightlifting. I'm eating healthily and spending more time with Ivy. I don't stare at my social media quite so much. I'm really, really trying. My therapist says I need to forgive myself for my mistakes, and I can't cling onto the guilt that eats away at me.

My hand moves to my stomach, and I draw strength from the life that's growing inside me.

A gremlin pokes his head out from the recesses of my mind, his giggles echoing off my skull.

Guilty, guilty, guilty. Your baby could get the disease, too. Did you think of that when you decided to get pregnant?

Squeezing my eyes shut, I try to talk myself down. The baby was an accident, but also a gift. I wouldn't be as dedicated to my recovery if I didn't have a child to take care of.

I *will* be a good mother, Huntington's or not.

"You okay, Margot?" Prince Luca glances at me, and I realize I'm gripping the edge of the stainless steel counter with both hands. My knuckles are white.

I force myself to relax my shoulders, painting a smile on my face. "I'm fine. Just a little dizzy, is all. Might need a muffin to keep me going."

"I never thought I'd see the day when you actually eat the things I bake," Ivy laughs, grabbing a banana chocolate-chip muffin from a tray for me. "It makes me happy to see you eating my stuff."

"You're a rare talent," I answer, taking a nibble of the muffin and groaning as the taste hits my tongue. "I can't believe I've been missing out on all this goodness just in the name of being skinny."

Ivy grins, then takes a deep breath. Her eyes shine as she stares at me. "Will you come open the doors with me? It's time. I want you beside me."

My heart thumps, and I nod. "I'd be honored."

We open the doors to the bakery together, smiling for the cameras that are waiting to snap photos of us. I hook my arm around my sister's shoulders, pointing to the sign above our heads.

Spoonful of Sugar is officially re-open for business.

This time, I'm happy about it.

The gremlins in my mind are blissfully quiet. The

anxious thoughts that plague me all the time are absent, and I'm truly, completely happy for my sister.

Ivy opens the front door to our house, and I glance up from my seat on the couch. Melissa, my hair stylist, is working on my blonde hair extensions, moving the wefts up closer to my scalp. She's been by my side for years, and is the closest thing I have to a friend.

"How was the rest of the grand re-opening?" I ask my sister.

Ivy smiles sweetly. "It was great. Lots of press. It meant a lot to me that you were there."

"You're such a star, Ivy," Mel says, tugging a strand of my hair.

I wince.

"Sorry," she says, patting the sore spot. She glances at my sister. "I tried one of your salted caramel brownies today. Oh. My. Lord. Ivy, you're incredible."

Ivy blushes, nodding. "Thank you."

"Let me do your hair this weekend," Mel says. "Take it as payment for all the baked goods you've fed me over the years."

"This?" Ivy says, flicking her black hair over her shoulder. "I don't know what you could do with this."

"Don't underestimate her," I grin, glancing at my hair stylist. "If she can make me into a long-haired blonde, she can make you feel like a princess."

Ivy's smile widens. "Well, okay. I'd like that."

My heart squeezes. Ivy is so...*good*. She's spent her whole life being by my side, not asking for anything. She's supported me through years of fame, never holding my status as a celebrity against me.

Me, though?

I resented her. When she opened her bakery, I thought she was using me and leaving me behind, just like everyone else.

It wasn't until she was hospitalized that I realized what an ass I was being.

The gremlins cackle in my mind, amplifying my insecurities.

You're a horrible person, and you don't deserve a sister like Ivy.

My sister flops down on the couch, letting out a long sigh. "Thank you for your help. I couldn't have re-opened the bakery without you."

I put my arm around my sister's shoulders. "Of course you could've. I didn't do anything except say the truth—that you're the best damn baker Farcliff has ever seen."

Ivy blushes. She's never been good at receiving compliments.

Melissa zhuzhes my hair one last time, and then pats my shoulder. "I've got to go. Keep that wrapped in a silk scarf while you sleep."

I give my friend a kiss on each cheek and watch her walk out through the front door. Glancing at myself in the reflection of the window, I let out a breath.

Melissa makes me look like a movie star, but inside, I still feel broken.

From the seat beside me, Ivy stares at me with those two-toned eyes of hers. One blue, one green. Just like our mother. I hold her gaze for a moment, and then I have to look away. Looking at my sister's face is too much like looking at Mama's.

Thinking of Mama makes me think of her death. Her death makes me think of my own diagnosis.

I wasn't even there when our mother died. I was on a photo shoot for Vogue Magazine.

What kind of person does that? Chooses work instead of family?

The rational part of my brain tries to stop the whirlwind of anxiety that threatens to drag me down. Logic tells me that it was my father who pushed me to work so much. He would guilt-trip me into taking more jobs, saying that the only way we could afford Mama's treatment was due to the money I made modeling and acting.

When you're just a young teenager, and your father says those kinds of things to you, you believe him. Being the main breadwinner for your family at age fourteen has a way of twisting your view of the world.

But even as I say those things to myself, the gremlins in my mind gather together and laugh at me.

Stop making excuses, they sneer. *You're just bad, bad, bad.*

Ivy takes a deep breath, pulling me from my thoughts. "You still don't want to tell me who the father is?"

She nods to my belly. My heart clenches. "It's not important."

"It *is* important, Margot," Ivy says softly. "Does he know, whoever he is?"

I shake my head. Ivy sighs.

I bite the inside of my cheek until I taste blood. I know exactly when I fell pregnant, and I know who the father is: Prince Beckett of Argyle. The man who tried to kill his half-brother, Prince Luca. The man who's currently on the run and has the entire Kingdom of Argyle looking for him.

I found out about my pregnancy when I was at the retreat. The doctor who told me was gentle and kind, but it didn't stop me feeling like the world was ending. Only Ivy and Luca know that I'm carrying a child—and the doctors, of course—and it still doesn't quite feel real.

My pregnancy is more fodder for the snarling voices in my mind.

What if I hurt my baby by injecting my body full of poison before I knew about the pregnancy? What if he or she doesn't develop properly because of what I've done?

What if the baby gets Huntington's?

Taking a deep breath, I reel my mind back in. My therapist tells me to name my anxiety, to treat it like an intruder in my mind. So, I try.

Those thoughts aren't serving me. Instead, I turn my mind inward, to the child growing inside me. Before I found out I was pregnant, I was only in that facility because I thought I needed to be. My anxiety was out of control, and I was afraid I'd do something to hurt myself. I didn't know how I overdosed, but I'm sure it was my own fault.

Guilty, guilty, guilty.

Once I found out I was pregnant, everything changed.

Now, I could never relapse. I could never do anything to willingly hurt my child. Never, ever, ever.

But Prince Beckett...

Maybe we're made for each other.

Bad, bad, bad.

"Have you taken your medication today?" Ivy asks.

I smile at my sister. "It's probably time for me to take it. Thanks for reminding me."

"I can see those wheels turning in your head. You need to stop torturing yourself."

"Easier said than done."

Ivy smiles sadly, wrapping her arms around me. "Everything will work out. That's what Luca always tells me. So far, he hasn't been wrong."

I nod, forcing a smile, but I know the truth. As soon as people find out I'm pregnant and who the father is, my career will be over. I'll lose my endorsements, and I doubt I'll ever land another acting gig.

Then, my body will slowly break down over the next ten, fifteen, twenty years.

I'm staring at the face of the grim reaper.

Everything will most definitely *not* work out.

2

DANTE

As soon as I step off the plane, my teeth start clacking. Cold air whips through my thin jacket and chills me to the bone.

It's not often that I leave the tropical, Caribbean island of Argyle—especially not to come up to somewhere as far north as Farcliff. Nestled between the United States and Canada, just east of the Great Lakes, Farcliff is a stunning country. Lush forests, clear lakes and rivers, healthy wildlife. Farcliff looks like a postcard brought to life.

But damn, it's cold—and it's not even November yet.

A driver is waiting next to a luxury sedan. He opens the back door for me, nodding as I slide into the car. I lean back, thankful for heated seats.

The driver gets in, glancing in the rear-view mirror. "Where to, Your Highness?"

I give him the address that Luca provided and then settle in for the drive. I don't often leave Argyle, so being driven to a strange address in a foreign Kingdom is a rare occurrence for me.

I'm on a recovery mission. Get Luca out of Farcliff and bring him back home.

Since I've always hated being in the public eye, King Theo of Argyle, my brother, has given me different responsibilities. I'm able to stay away from the cameras as long as I deal with most of the day-to-day goings-on in Argyle. That leaves him free to travel to other countries and Kingdoms, work on international relations, and be the face of Argyle.

It helps that I've always been good with computers. I developed a state-of-the-art security system for the Argyle Palace, upgrading everything tech-related on our royal premises. Now that Beckett is on the run, I'm glad that my family is safe. No one except a select few people know that I'm the one behind the upgrades to the security in the Palace.

Anonymity has its advantages.

For one, I don't get mobbed if I go outside the palace gates. I can travel unhindered, and I don't have to deal with lies and stories about me in the media. They call me the 'reclusive prince,' but I don't mind.

I *am* a recluse.

Another advantage is a situation like this one. With our half-brother Beckett on the run, there are precious few people that we can trust. Theo sent me to Farcliff to bring Luca back to our home Kingdom of Argyle. He'll be safer at home.

Luca's girlfriend just re-opened her bakery, but I'm hoping I can convince him to choose safety and common sense. We don't know who we can trust in Farcliff, so it's better if they both come back to Argyle.

Typically, I wouldn't leave my home Kingdom, but things are tense back home, and I was the only one who could make the trip without causing a splash in the media.

Since my face isn't plastered over every media outlet in the world, and few people know what I actually look like, the task to bring Luca home has fallen to me.

I watch the streets of Farcliff whizz by. People walk quickly with their chins stuffed in their jackets against the cold. It's getting dark already, and the days are only getting shorter. I'd rather be on a tropical island, that's for sure.

The driver pulls up outside a tall gate. I can just see the top of a house behind a row of trees. He rolls his window down and reaches for the buzzer, exchanging a few words with a security guard. The gates swing inward, and I'm taken up the driveway to my temporary new home.

Hopefully it has good heating and insulation.

Stepping outside, I nod to the driver as he takes my bag out of the trunk. "I'll take it from here," I say.

"Are you sure, Your Highness?" He hesitates, not wanting to hand the suitcase over.

In Argyle, all the staff in the castle is used to me. I don't like being coddled or treated like...well, like royalty. I dress myself, I drive myself, I do most thing without the help of my staff.

This driver obviously isn't used to that. I smile at him, slipping some money into his hand as a tip before grabbing my suitcase. I packed light, because I don't own any cold weather clothes, and I don't intend to be here long.

If Luca will listen to reason, I'm hoping we can get out of here at the break of dawn tomorrow and be back in the sunshine and warmth by noon.

Easy, right?

Setting my small suitcase on the front porch, I ring the doorbell. I take a step back, clasping my hands behind me as I wait for the door to open.

Light, quick footsteps approach on the other side. The lock slides, and the heavy door swings inward.

My breath catches.

I've seen pictures of Margot LeBlanc. I've seen her in half a dozen films, and I respect her skills as an actor.

But, damn. Cameras do *not* do her justice.

I guess a part of me just assumed that it was Photoshop. I didn't think she'd actually be this breathtaking in person.

Her long, waist-length blonde hair is swept to one side. Bright blue eyes stare back at me, and her full, kissable lips fall open. She drags her eyes down my body and back up again, and I'm surprised at how much I enjoy her gaze.

Heat follows her eyes, sending little tendrils of pleasure snaking through my veins. I let a grin tug at my lips, arching an eyebrow.

Margot's almost as tall as I am, with a thin waist and gorgeous curves. My eyes keep wanting to drop down to her body, but it's her eyes that are magnetic. Deep pools of blue stare back at me.

I clear my throat, but I still can't seem to make words.

This is why I don't go out. This is why I hate the public eye. I clam up.

Margot's face breaks into a polite smile. "You must be Todd," she says. "Thank you for coming on such short notice."

I frown. Who's Todd?

Before I can answer, Margot slides some slippers on her feet and motions for me to follow her. We head around the house, and my eyes stay glued to the movement of her ass. She glances over her shoulder, and my eyes snap up to hers.

"Is your truck out on the street? I'll let security know to let you in. I thought I mentioned you were coming, but it's been so busy with my sister's bakery re-opening that it must have slipped my mind."

"Uh, no, actually. They let me in."

Because I'm the Prince of Argyle and I'm here to see my brother.

"Oh, good," she smiles. "Here's the pool. I think the pump is burned out. It just won't turn on. The electricity went out yesterday, and I think there was a power surge when it came back on. I'm not an electrician, though. You are," she laughs, the sound sending another wave of heat through me. "We're hoping to drain a few inches off it this week to get it ready for winter, but my house manager was saying it would be best to have you take a look at it before we take too much water out."

Her smile is polite. Guarded. She points to a waist-high wooden box, flipping open the lid to reveal the pool pump.

"You think you can fix it?"

"Dante!" My brother Luca throws open the sliding glass door and strides out of the house. His smile stretches from ear to ear.

He looks happier than he did even a couple of weeks ago when I saw him in Argyle. Maybe the cold weather suits him.

Maybe Ivy suits him.

Margot makes a soft noise. "Dante?"

I glance at her, smiling. "Yeah."

Luca bounds around the pool and wraps his arms around me, engulfing me in a hug. "Good to see you, brother."

"Brother?" Margot repeats, her eyes widening. A blush stains her cheeks as horror fills her eyes.

"Margot, this is my brother, Prince Dante of Argyle. Don't be fooled by his size, though. He's a shy little teddy bear."

Luca wraps me in a headlock and rubs his knuckles over my head. I yelp, trying to spin away from him, but my brother won't let go. I shift my weight, trying to push him off me.

His arm stays firmly wrapped around my neck, gently crushing my airway.

Panic starts to lace my blood. I don't like being trapped.

I try to get away from his grip again, pushing a little bit harder.

Too hard.

We stumble back, stepping over each other's feet as we both head toward the edge of the pool. Luca laughs, grunting as he struggles with me.

My brother's gotten stronger since we were kids.

Margot takes a step toward us. "Uh, boys..."

With one massive push, I try to get Luca off me. He yelps, letting go of my neck as he falls backward, pitching toward the pool water. His eyes open wide as his heel slips over the edge of the pool.

He's a goner. In a second, he'll be splashing into ice-cold water.

Taking a step back, I suck in a wheezing breath. I put my hand to my throat, finally filling my lungs.

My victory is short-lived, though, because with one last movement, Luca grabs onto my shoulder and drags me down with him.

I yell, falling into the freezing-cold water on top of my brother. The cold takes my breath away. For a second, I can't move. I just sink down, down, down, until my knee hits the bottom of the pool. The feeling of the bottom jars me back to my senses.

I push away from Luca and propel myself off the bottom, breaking the surface to hear Margot shouting. She disappears into the pool house. I swim to the edge of the pool and watch Margot come back out carrying a bundle of towels.

I pull myself out of the water, my clothes soaked and my mood dampened. Luca's head pops up above the water, laughing.

He's in a pretty good mood, considering our half-brother

Beckett just tried to kill him. Does he think I'm here on a social visit?

A black-haired girl appears in the doorway. "What the heck is going on?"

Margot hands me a towel, arching an eyebrow. Her cheeks are still a bright shade of red, and she averts her eyes.

"Babe! This is my brother, Dante," Luca calls out. "You should get in here. The water's nice."

"I'll take your word for it," Ivy answers, laughing.

My whole body is shaking. I don't realize it until Margot drapes a towel over my shoulders and rubs her hands up and down my arms.

"Let's get you inside," she says, glancing at Luca, who's still trying to get Ivy to jump in. "You're obviously more sensible than your older brother."

"It would appear that way," I grin. My teeth chatter, and Margot nods toward the house.

As soon as I step inside, pins and needles erupt over my body. Heat starts seeping into my frozen skin, and Margot leads me up the stairs.

"Bathroom, bedroom." She points to two different doors. "There should be clean towels and toiletries in the bathroom. Warm yourself up. You have a suitcase?"

"On the front porch."

She nods. "I'll get someone to bring it up and leave it in that room."

"Thanks." I swallow, wanting to say something else.

Her eyes linger on mine for a moment, and then she inhales sharply. "And, uh...sorry."

"For what?"

"For thinking you were the electrician, and not the Prince of Argyle."

I chuckle, shrugging. "Easy mistake to make."

Margot's eyes drift over my chest, and I watch her cheeks flush brighter. She smiles shyly, nodding as she turns back toward the stairs.

I watch her for a moment, wondering why my heart is beating so erratically.

3

MARGOT

FOR FARCLIFF'S SAKE, of course I would do something like that. Who else would mistake literal *royalty* for a pool technician?

No one, that's who. Just graceful ol' me.

My cheeks are still burning when I make my way downstairs. Ivy's in the pool with Luca now, and the two of them are kissing like no one's watching.

I let out a sigh, turning to the kitchen.

My hands shake as I grab a glass of water, trying to let go of the nervousness that seems to have settled deep in the pit of my stomach.

Is that nervousness, or is it another tremor?

I push the thought away. The more I think about my disease, the more I worry about it. My mind turns back to Dante, in all his soaking wet, muscled glory. The image of him pulling himself out of the pool will stay burned in my mind for a long, long time.

It's not often that a man has that effect on me. I've been around lots of famous people, lots of gorgeous men, lots of people with money and clout...

...but no one like Prince Dante.

I lean against the kitchen counter, squeezing my eyes shut.

There goes any hope of sleeping tonight. I already know I'll replay that interaction over and over again, torturing myself with the absolute mortifying shame of it all. The last half hour of my life will probably play on repeat in my head for the next ten years.

Even the way Prince Dante looked at me when we were upstairs—with that sexy, pouty smirk—made me burn with embarrassment...and something else.

Desire.

Treacherous, forbidden desire.

How could I even consider being attracted to him, when I'm carrying another man's baby? No, not just another man. I'm carrying his horrible half-brother's baby.

Great.

I sink down on a stool and lean my elbows on the kitchen island.

Maybe it's hormonal. They say that pregnancy can pique your libido. I'm well into the second trimester, now, and I rarely feel nauseous. I have way more energy.

Maybe my body is just looking for a way to burn it off?

For example, I could burn it off by climbing Prince Dante like a tree. I'm sure he could find a way to get rid of a lot of excess energy with me.

Just an idea.

I'm not going to act on it.

I jump when someone clears their throat in the kitchen doorway. My eyes widen when I see Prince Dante in nothing but a towel. My eyes drift down his chiseled body, feasting on the sight before me.

Muscle. Brawn. Sex-god status.

A little droplet of water escapes his hair and starts trailing down his body. Fascinated, I watch its journey from his collarbone, over his chest, and down the center valley of his abdominal muscles. The adventurous drop of water makes it all the way to his towel, absorbing into the fluffy white fabric just as my eyes snap back up to his.

Did I mention my cheeks are on fire?

The Prince arches an eyebrow. "Did you happen to grab my suitcase?"

"Oh!" I clap my hand over my mouth. "I'm so sorry. I was distracted by...stuff..." I shake my head, trying to keep my eyes from finding more droplets of water trailing down his body.

His hand is holding the towel up, and a fleeting image of the Prince dropping it passes through my mind. I clear my throat, shaking my head to dispel the thought.

Bad Margot.

Blame the hormones.

I avert my eyes from his brawn, rushing past him and taking care not to touch his body as I slip through the kitchen entrance. I make my way to the front door, hauling in his suitcase.

"Here," I say.

One of the house staff appears and rushes forward to help with the bag. She takes it from me and starts hauling it up the staircase.

The Prince's eyes stay glued on mine, and I do my best to keep my gaze above shoulder level. Heat teases the edges of my stomach, and my heart thumps.

My tongue slides out to moisten my lips, but my mind feels completely empty. I scramble to think of something to say—anything.

Anything at all.

Earth to Margot? Where have you gone? Say something!

Where did my brain go? Did it go on a long journey with that droplet of water? Why am I suddenly mute?

The Prince clears his throat. "I'd better..."

"Yeah," I say, averting my gaze. "I'll see you..."

"Thanks..."

"Uh-huh."

We stumble over each other's words until the Prince coughs into his fist and turns around.

I cringe hard, releasing a breath as soon as I hear his bedroom door close.

Why am I like this?

I swear, I'm the worst famous person in the world. I somehow missed the classes on poise and grace, and hung onto my core awkwardness.

Hunter used to say it's what made me relatable, and part of the reason that I've been as successful as I've been. People see me, and they recognize themselves.

I just wish people didn't love a cringey, awkward mess. Do normal people knock things over every single day? Do normal people think *Dante of Freaking Argyle* is actually Todd the Plumber?!

Just another thing for my anxious brain to obsess over in the middle of the night, I guess. Add it to the long list of material that I already have.

A few months ago, Ivy and I ended up on a yacht with Prince Beckett, Prince Luca, and a bunch of celebrities. I fell in the water, and Ivy had to jump in to save me. It was all over the news for days. I laughed it off, but I died a thousand times every time I saw a photo of me flailing in the water.

That little episode has been playing on repeat in my mind every night, so at least now I'll have something new to cringe about when I can't sleep.

My phone chimes from the living room, and I release a heavy sigh.

It'll be some notification of another news story about me.

Hunter used to tell me that all publicity was good publicity. Now, I just find it all exhausting. It makes me wonder what else Hunter did to keep me on top. What other crimes were committed in my name?

My phone lights up again, and I turn away in disgust.

I once compared being famous to being locked up in a high tower, with no doors or stairs leading up to the top. I can see life as it's lived for everyone else—for people like Ivy and her friends, Giselle and Georgina. They can lead normal lives. They can go through their happiness and sadness in private, finding joy in whatever pockets of life they choose to look.

I don't even know how I got up here. The tower is luxurious, don't get me wrong. I'm grateful for all the money that I've earned, and all the boxes of gifts that I'm sent every single day. I'm grateful for the fast track at the airport, and the private cars and jets that take me wherever I need to go.

I'm not wanting for anything...

...except genuine connection.

The only people I can truly trust are Ivy and my hair stylist Melissa. Ivy was the only one who was strong enough to walk away from me when I was being self-destructive. Melissa is the only person, other than Ivy, who was fully supportive of my three-month retreat.

Ivy ended up poisoned because of her connection to me.

Because of *me*.

Another ding sounds from my phone, and I march over to it with a huff. Without looking at the screen, I turn it on silent and put it on a high shelf.

I can't look at it right now.

Ever since I've gotten back to Farcliff, the media have all wanted a piece of me. I'm supposed to do an exclusive exposé with one of the main media outlets in Farcliff next week. The 'tell-all' interview that will have people salivating at the thought of my shortcomings.

My publicist has been contacting me non-stop. My most lucrative brand sponsorship—with a haircare company, on account of my trademark blonde locks—is on the rocks. I touch my head, itching at the base of my hair extensions.

All I want to do is rip them out. I'd get rid of my blonde hair in an instant, but that would mean risking my image and my career.

I have to do the tell-all interview, prove myself worthy of being sponsored, and then life can go on as normal.

Except for this little problem growing in my uterus. I won't exactly be the model spokeswoman for mental health, recovery, and redemption when I have Prince Beckett's baby growing inside me.

No—calling my child a problem is wrong. My baby is a gift. This baby gives me more strength than I can say, and provides me with a ladder that I can use to climb down from the tower where I've held myself captive.

With a child, I'll be a mother. Nothing else. Not a famous actress, not a former model, not a celebrity or a socialite.

I'll be a mom.

What's more beautiful than that?

I slink out the front door and let my feet take me to the edge of my property. I peer through the fence at the world beyond, wondering what it would be like to be normal.

What if I didn't have the weight of the world's expectations on my shoulders?

What if I hadn't been made to provide for my entire family when I was just a kid?

What if I'd had a normal childhood?

I glance behind me at the big, luxurious house, and I sigh.

I wouldn't have all that. There wouldn't be two princes living with me, and Ivy would never have met the love of her life.

As trapped as I feel, I have to stay grateful.

Ivy got off the hamster wheel. She's chasing her dream with the bakery. She isn't attached to me anymore, and she's living her life the way she wants to.

Maybe I can do the same.

My hand slides over my abdomen, and a smile drifts over my lips.

This baby will change everything.

4

DANTE

LUCA EMERGES from a bedroom across the hall at the same time as I walk out of mine.

I nod to him. "I need to talk to you."

"News from Argyle?"

"More like lack of news."

Luca grunts, gesturing down the stairs. He leads me to a small study at the back of the mansion. There are messy stacks of papers on a desk beside a photo of Margot and Ivy when they were little girls. I pick up the photo, staring at the open-mouthed laugh on Margot's frozen face.

There's a lightness in her eyes that I didn't see in her today.

That's what growing older in the public eye does, I guess. Dims your smile. I've seen it in Theo, in Luca, and even in Beckett. They've all spent their lives in front of the cameras, under intense scrutiny, and they've all become more guarded than they were before.

I saw it in my parents. It tore my mother and father apart, and it might be the reason my mother, the Queen, went to look for love in other places. Like the King's brother's bed.

Shaking my head, I bring myself back to the present. Now is not the time to dwell on the past. I put the photo back down and turn to look at my brother. Luca arches an eyebrow.

"So? What's the news?"

I take a deep breath. "Beckett is still in the wind. Theo has upped security at all the airports and ports, but he could have slipped away from Argyle already. The truth is, we don't know where he is."

Luca nods. Our half-brother was here in Farcliff with Luca, and we've just discovered that he attempted to swap out Luca's painkillers for dangerously powerful drugs. Had Luca taken them, he would almost certainly have overdosed.

"Still no idea why he wanted to kill you?" I ask.

Luca sighs, slumping down onto a chair. "When he attacked me..." He shakes his head. "He just said he'd been jealous of me. Said he loved Cara and thought she would start seeing him after I was injured. He didn't like seeing me with Margot."

"But you were never with Margot." My voice is hard. I frown, not liking the pang that shoots through my chest.

Luca shakes his head. "Nah. It was all just publicity, like I was supposed to do. Ivy's always been the one."

I nod, the tension in my shoulders easing.

Am I jealous?

"Theo wants me to bring you home," I say after a pause.

Luca arches an eyebrow. "Are you Theo's little lapdog now? You go and fetch for him?"

I roll my eyes. "Don't be an idiot, Luca. You'll be safer in Argyle. The systems we've developed are world-class. Here in Farcliff, we're exposed."

"I can't leave Ivy. Beckett knows how much I care about

her, and if he really wants to hurt me, the easiest way to do it is through her. I have to stay."

"So, bring her. Let's go back to Argyle together."

"Why is it safer there?" His eyebrows draw together. "If they think Beckett is still in Argyle, wouldn't it be safer for us to stay here?"

"We don't know where he is, Luca," I explain. "And we don't know who to trust here."

Luca lets out a sigh, shaking his head. "No. I'm not going back. Ivy just re-opened the bakery. We have to stay. And if she's here, I'm here. That's non-negotiable. Let Beckett come here and try to kill me again."

I turn away from him, crossing my arms. Staring out the window, I try to find the words to explain what I'm thinking. Luca spent five years away from Argyle. I went from having my best friend and brother at my side every day, to not even seeing him once.

After the accident that broke his back, Luca spent years recovering in Singapore. He refused to let us come visit him.

I missed him. Now, I want him to come home.

But when I look at my brother again, I see a different man. He picks up the same photo that I'd been looking at, and his eyes soften.

I know he's not looking at Margot's laughing face. He's looking at Ivy.

Luca's in love.

My brother has always been fiercely loyal. He loved Cara, now our Queen, from the time he was five or six years old. Growing up, I always thought they'd end up together.

When she married Theo, I thought Luca would never come back home.

But he did. He loves Argyle. He loves our family...

...and now, he loves Ivy, too.

I have to respect that.

I nod, making a decision. "I'm staying too, then."

Luca's eyebrow arches. "What?"

"I'm staying with you."

"Wouldn't you be safer in Argyle?"

"Maybe," I say. "But I...I care about you, Luca." A lump forms in my throat. It's not often that we talk to each other like this, but I need to get the words out. "I missed you. And I'm not going to leave you here on your own to fend for yourself. At least if I'm here, we can both watch over the bakery. We can keep an eye on each other's backs for any sign of Beckett. I can help."

Luca gulps, standing up. He stares at me. "You would do that?"

I chuckle. "I'm not *that* much of a hermit."

"You haven't spent more than a few days away from Argyle since you were ten."

I grin. "Okay, maybe I am that much of a hermit. I just don't like being in the public eye. It's not for me."

"The media in Farcliff are vultures. If they catch wind that you're here..."

"I'll take that chance. I've spent the past couple of decades staying out of the public eye. I think I can do it here, too."

"You'd do that for me?"

I nod, not trusting my voice. I've spent so much time away from Luca that it feels right to stay here with him. He needs me more than Theo does. Our King is surrounded by the castle walls and thousands of palace guards.

In a way, I feel like Luca deserves Ivy's love. He should stay here and be happy with her, if that's what he wants. He went through the most horrible accident I could imagine, broke his back, learned to walk again, was betrayed by the woman he loved, only to find someone who he loves even more.

I'll stand by him.

Before I can react, Luca wraps his arms around me in a bone-crushing hug. He lifts my feet off the ground—not an easy feat, considering I'm an inch taller than him—and sets me back down with a thud.

When he pulls away, Luca's eyes are misty. "Thank you, Dante."

"I'll call Theo to let him know."

I give him a smile and turn toward the door, pausing when I reach it. I glance over my shoulder. "You got any clothes I can borrow? I only brought one sweater, and I don't think it'll do much against the cold."

Luca laughs, nodding. "Yeah, but you'd better not stretch it out. I'll get someone to buy you a winter wardrobe."

"Thanks." I grin at my brother.

When I walk out of the study, I let out a sigh. Something significant has shifted. I'm stepping out of my cocoon to be here. I'm going out on a limb to stay by my brother's side, and it might mean facing the public scrutiny. It might mean being photographed and talked about—especially considering I'm living with one of the most famous celebrities in the Kingdom.

But Luca's worth it. He's my brother, and I've been away from his side for too long. If my job is to keep him safe, then I'll have to do it from here.

I walk down the hallway just as the front door opens. Margot steps through, locking the door behind her. My eyes sweep over her curves, and I long to tangle my fingers in her long, golden hair.

Maybe a small part of me wanted to stay for her, too. It's

been a long, long time since I've met a woman who can make me feel the way she does.

As if she senses my stare, Margot turns around and meets my gaze. Heat floods my body from my head down to my toes, swirling around my chest and landing somewhere in the pit of my stomach. My veins ignite, and every bit of my body wants to get closer to her.

The actress gives me a small curtsy as she blushes.

I frown. "What are you doing?"

"Curtsying, Your Highness."

My frown deepens. "Curtsying? Your Highness?" I fight the grin off my face. "Ma'am, you have me mistaken for someone else. I'm Todd. I just fixed your pool pump."

5

MARGOT

I WOULD LAUGH HARDER if I wasn't so mortified. I giggle, covering my eyes with my hand.

"Don't make me re-live that," I groan.

The Prince chuckles, walking toward me. "You don't have to curtsy every time you see me, Margot. I'm living in your house."

I drag my gaze up to meet his, and a dagger of heat pierces my stomach, staying lodged deep in my center. Gulping, I nod. "Okay."

The Prince nods to the door behind me. "Everything okay out there?"

The way Prince Dante's eyebrows draw together makes me feel like he really cares. His shoulders straighten, and as he closes the distance between us, I feel safer than I've felt in a long time. The persistent, nagging feeling that something bad is going to happen fades away, and I'm able to breathe easier.

I nod. "Yeah. I just needed some air."

"I'm not that bad, am I?" Prince Dante's eyebrow arches. "I hope you won't need air every time you talk to me."

I blush. I didn't realize I'm a blusher, but apparently the Prince brings out the worst in me.

"You're not bad at all."

The Prince's eyes linger on mine. His tongue slides out to lick his lips, and my heart stutters. Raking his fingers through his hair, Prince Dante lets out a sigh.

Does he know how incredibly handsome he is? Every movement he makes is strong, purposeful, magnetic. Every look he gives me sends lava coursing through my veins. Every time I catch a whiff of his cologne, my heart skips a beat.

It doesn't even look like he's trying, but pretty soon I'm going to need a 'Wet Floor' sign whenever I'm around him.

The Prince clears his throat. "I hope you don't mind, I spoke to Luca. Looks like I'll be spending more time than anticipated here in Farcliff. There are...things...that worry us, and it's best for me to stay here."

"Beckett?" I ask as my heart sinks. Any reminder of the father of my child sends dread creeping into my heart.

Prince Dante's shoulders fall. He nods. "You know about that?"

"I only know that he tried to hurt Luca—Prince Luca, I mean—but not much else."

Prince Dante grins. "You can call him Luca. I do. You can call me Dante, too. If I'm living under your roof, I think it's only fair we be comfortable with each other."

My blush deepens. The thought of being *comfortable* with Prince Dante has crossed my mind more than once in the past hour.

Where did I put that 'Wet Floor' sign, again? Might as well get it ready.

"How long will you stay?" My voice squeaks, and I clear my throat to cover the noise.

"As long as I need to."

There's only a foot of space between us, and I desperately want to erase it. My fingers itch to feel the curve of his shoulders. To sink into the hard brawn of his muscle. To feel the heat of his skin under mine.

Swallowing the thoughts down, I force a smile. "I should go to bed. Please let me know if you need anything."

The Prince nods, and I sidestep my way around his broad body, feeling his gaze on my back as I make my way up the stairs.

Turns out, I was right when I thought I wouldn't sleep tonight, but I'm not reliving any mortifying incidents from the past ten years. I'm just replaying the sight of Prince Dante standing in my kitchen in nothing but a towel. When I close my eyes, I imagine how it would have felt to catch that adventurous drop of water with my tongue.

That thought alone keeps me awake most of the night.

WHEN I GET UP, Luca and Ivy are already at the bakery. I retrieve my phone from the shelf in the living room, sighing when I see thirty-two missed calls from my publicist. As I stare at the screen, the phone flashes and her name appears. I press the green 'answer' button.

"Hi, Felicity."

"She's alive!" my publicist exclaims sarcastically.

"Sorry I missed your calls. There's been a lot going on."

"I know, Margot. And one of the more important things that's going on is your interview with the *Farcliff Observer*. You haven't forgotten, have you?"

My chest squeezes, and I force myself to take a full breath. "No, I haven't forgotten."

Even the thought of stepping in front of a camera makes

my pulse quicken. My fingers and toes suddenly feel ice-cold, and I sink down into a chair.

"The car will be there to pick you up at one o'clock. Hair and makeup will be arriving at your place at eleven, and they'll accompany you to the interview. I'll meet you there."

Felicity says a few more things that I barely hear, and then hangs up without waiting for an answer. I can feel her annoyance with me through the phone, and I wince when the phone disconnects.

"Everything okay?" I turn to see Dante at the edge of the living room. His dark hair is tousled, his eyes still a bit sleepy. He's wearing a plain white t-shirt and dark jeans. He doesn't look like a prince at all, but then again, I don't know why I expected princes to be formal all the time.

I release a breath and nod. "Yeah, everything's fine. I have an interview today that I've been dreading."

"I know what you mean," Dante grins.

"Not a fan of interviews?"

"Not even a little bit. I hate them. I've been lucky, though." Dante takes a step into the living room and sits down on one of the sofas. He stretches his legs out and crosses them at the ankle, looking completely comfortable in his own skin.

I envy the ease with which he carries himself. Sometimes, it feels like my entire existence is just one long, awkward struggle. Seeing people who just float through life makes me wish that I wasn't so anxious all the time.

I've always been this way, and in the past few months, every time my body trembles it makes me think that my disease is progressing.

The Prince takes a deep breath. "When I was a kid, a video of me went viral. I was sick, and I ended up throwing up all over my ceremonial uniform." Dante glances at me, shaking his head. "It seems so pathetic to say that now, but it really scarred me."

"I get that."

"It was at a time when there were things going on between my mother, my father, and my uncle." He inhales, shaking his head. "Things got out of control, and I just decided that the public eye wasn't for me. The throwing up was just the straw that broke the camel's back, really."

Dante pinches his lips.

"It was back in the day when 'viral' really meant *viral*. Not now, where anytime a video gets a few thousand views, they say it's viral. In those days, a viral video meant that *everyone* had seen it. Nearly everyone in the world has seen me blow chunks on my little ten-year-old's ceremonial uniform."

"I would definitely replay that until the end of my days," I laugh. "It would keep me up at night for years."

"It got really bad when I was eleven or twelve. My mother had run off with my uncle, and she'd tried to take me with her. It was a mess. I was afraid to go out in case someone made fun of me." Dante grimaces. "I just cracked. I couldn't handle it. The rest of my family were really understanding. They let me work in the background, and my face hasn't been that publicized. Luca stepped forward, as did Theo. People still know who I am, but I'm not nearly as recognizable as they are."

I grin. "I can attest to that...Todd."

"I'll admit, *that* was a first." Dante smiles. He nods his chin toward me. "What's your interview?"

I blow the air out of my lungs, shaking my head. "An exclusive interview about my overdose, anxiety, and recovery. 'Margot LeBlanc bares it all.' I'm supposed to be vulnerable and open and win back my audience with my candor. Or so my publicist says."

"That's the stuff of nightmares."

"Don't remind me. I'll just try to get through it. It'll be my first time in front of the cameras since…" I take a deep breath. "Since I left for the retreat."

"Is there anything I can do?"

I smile sadly. "I don't think so. I just have to prepare myself for the internet trolls who talk about how much weight I've gained, and how my agent dumped me, and how my sponsorships are falling through. You think you have thick skin until you read comments online."

Dante laughs. "Just try not to throw up on yourself. I can say from experience that the comments on *that* video are vicious."

"I'll keep that in mind." I stand up, smiling at the Prince. "Have you had breakfast yet?"

As Dante follows me into the kitchen, I'm surprised to note that the tension in my body has eased. The Prince offers to make pancakes.

"I won't say no to a prince cooking for me," I say, sliding onto a bar stool at the kitchen island.

Prince Dante smiles, spinning around in the kitchen and opening cupboards to look for a pan. I watch him as my heart eases and the panic that had started to mount inside me fades away.

Shockingly, the Prince can cook. He makes me laugh and forget all about my interview for a few hours.

By the time Melissa and my makeup artist arrive at the house, I'm relaxed and confident, and I haven't let my own mind sabotage me…

…yet.

When Melissa turns the corner and flashes a smile at me, I relax even more.

"Come on, gorgeous. Let's get you ready."

I follow my friend into the bedroom and sit down where she directs me. She wiggles her eyebrows at me in the mirror.

"Who was that hunk in the kitchen?"

"No one." I try to hide my grin.

"Didn't look like no one." She winks at me, and another blush warms my cheeks. Melissa clicks her tongue, grinning at me in the mirror. "Look at you, getting back on the horse. I'm proud of you."

I force a smile as my thoughts flick to the baby inside me. Getting 'back on the horse' doesn't seem like such a great idea for me right now.

"I think you need a good orgasm," Melissa says, focused on my hair. "Something to take your mind off things. When was the last time a man like that made you come?"

I force a smile, laughing awkwardly in response.

The truth? Years. I haven't actually had pleasure from sex or intimacy in a long, long time. Before sleeping with Prince Beckett, it had been over a year since I'd had sex.

A part of me thinks that maybe orgasms just aren't a part of my life anymore. Maybe that ship has sailed. Pleasure has been replaced with anxiety.

But as my thoughts flick to Dante, and the way he makes my body burn, I think that maybe Melissa is right. Maybe it's time for me to let my hair down.

6

DANTE

MARGOT IS WHISKED AWAY by her team, and re-emerges looking like a different person. Gone are the soft, subtle lines of her face. Instead, she looks glamorous and done up. Her long, blonde hair is carefully curled and swept to one side in a natural, effortless kind of way.

Holding her arms out, she grins at me. "Ta-da!"

Honestly, Margot could wear a paper bag and she would look incredible. Hanging out with her this morning made me realize that she's not just a vapid celebrity.

"You look beautiful," I say. It's the truth. 'Beautiful' doesn't even cover it, but gushing about how fucking hard she's making me doesn't seem like the right thing to do. My heart thumps as I try to swallow past a lump in my throat.

Margot smiles, blushing. The thought of her blushing at a compliment is funny to me, in a way. I'm sure she gets showered with praise all day, every day—and yet my words have that effect on her.

The team rushes around her, touching up her hair as she walks toward the front door. I nod to her, and something tugs at my heart. Disappointment seeps into my chest as I watch her approach the front door.

Then, Margot pauses. Turning to face me, she tilts her head.

"Do you... Would you like to come?"

I frown. "Me?"

Margot blushes harder, shaking her head. "Stupid question. I know you must hate these things. I just thought... I don't know what I thought. I'll see you later."

"I'll come," I blurt out, grabbing Luca's jacket from the closet.

Margot's face brightens. "Really? You don't have to."

"I want to."

Surprisingly, it's the truth. We walk out to the waiting car, and I slide my hand over her lower back. Tingles flow up my arm, and my breath catches in my throat.

Margot exchanges a glance with one of her stylists—either hair or makeup—and her blush deepens.

When we get in the car, her soft, feminine scent fills my nostrils. I inhale, committing the smell to memory. It makes heat flood my stomach, and I force myself to calm my racing heart.

How is it possible for a woman to have this effect on me? I love it and hate it at the same time. I don't want to be around her when I feel tongue-tied and clumsy, but there's nowhere else I'd rather be.

"You sure you want to come? You look nervous."

"Only because I'm sitting next to you." I grin as if it's a joke. I haven't even thought about the fact that we're going to a TV studio, or that there will be cameras and microphones and interviewers all around.

Margot chuckles, but it dies quickly. She glances at the driver, and then leans toward me.

"I'm nervous."

I slide my hand into hers, giving it a squeeze. Margot's face softens, and a tentative smile spreads across her lips. She lets out a long breath, and nods slowly.

"Thank you."

We keep holding hands for the duration of the ride. I feel like I'm fourteen years old again, nervous to be around a girl I like. It feels right to have her palm against mine, but it makes my mind jump to all kinds of other situations.

Is my hand getting too sweaty? Can she see the tightening in my pants? Do I have food stuck in my teeth?

I steal a glance at Margot, and my heart takes off at breakneck speed again.

I imagine slipping her out of her sheer, white blouse and running my hands over her curves. I think about the fullness of her breasts, and how they swell with every breath.

My blood turns to fire and my whole body burns.

I want her. I can't deny it.

But it's something else, too. There's something about Margot that I wasn't expecting. There's a depth to her that doesn't come through in her public persona. She's fragile, and sensitive, and she cares deeply about her sister.

I glance at Margot, who chews her bottom lip as she stares out the window. This is her life—living in the public eye, dealing with interviews and public criticism. Having everyone give their opinion on her appearance, her character, her life, her choices.

I don't want to get involved with that world. Her life is exactly the one I've been avoiding since I was young. All my time staying secluded inside the palace walls and keeping my face out of the media has been to prevent my life from turning into hers.

She is the exact opposite of what I want.

So, why is my body betraying me whenever she's near?

Then, Margot turns to look at me, and flashes her brilliant smile. It sends an arrow straight through my chest, and I forget what I was worried about a second ago.

We stop outside the studio, and Margot slips her hand out of mine. I miss her skin as soon as she pulls away. When we get out of the car, I can only smell faint whispers of her perfume, and I wish my face was buried in her hair.

I want to be closer.

We're taken to a dressing room, where a long table of snacks and drinks has been laid out. Margot ignores them all. She sits down in front of the mirror, fussing with her hair and taking deep breaths.

"You okay?" I ask.

She turns away from the mirror, shaking her head. "I don't know."

A knock sounds on the door, and we both turn our heads. "*They're ready for you,*" one of Margot's team says through the closed door.

All the blood drains from Margot's face. She gulps, nodding as if the person can see her. "Okay, be out in a minute." Margot's voice sounds strangled, and her chest starts to rise and fall. She's shaking. Her hands grip the edges of her seat as she starts breathing more and more rapidly, letting out short gasps.

I move toward Margot, kneeling in front of her. I put my hands on her thighs. "Margot, are you okay?"

"I can't..." she wheezes. "I can't..."

"Look at my eyes."

Margot looks at me, and sheer terror fills her eyes. "I can't breathe," she finally says. Her hands go to her neck, and panic starts to overtake her face. Margot's eyes dart from one end of the room to the other, and her body starts to rock back and forth.

I know what's happening, because I've been in her shoes. Not for many, many years, but I've been there.

She's having a panic attack.

"Margot, look at me." I keep my voice soft, but firm. She drags her eyes to mine. "I want you to slow down your breathing with me."

I inhale, counting to five, and exhale, counting to five. Margot tries her best to follow, her shaking breaths not quite lasting that long. We do that three or four times, and then I ask her to look at me again.

"Think about the feeling of the chair supporting you. Your breath as it passes through your nose. The warmth of my hands on your thighs."

Her hands move over mine and Margot nods, inhaling again. Her fingers curl around mine and she clings onto me as if I'm her lifeline. Next time we take a breath together, she's able to smooth her breath out. Her shoulders drop, and the trembling in her body grows more gentle.

We stay like that for a while. I have no idea how long. Seconds? Minutes?

I try to talk slowly, calmly, as if I were talking to a nervous animal. Margot's hands curl around my fingers, and she leans forward to rest her forehead against mine. We stay like that, eyes closed, breath mixing, until I feel the panic inside her ease.

Finally, she pulls away. Her eyes mist up, and she shakes her head.

"I'm sorry."

"Don't apologize."

"I'm embarrassed. I don't..." She bites her lip.

I cup her face in my hand, dragging my thumb over her

cheek. Her skin is so soft, her eyes so gentle, I wonder how someone like this could ever face the harshness of the public eye.

"I've been in your shoes," I say. "I know how you feel."

Margot nods, jumping when another knock sounds on the door. *"Margot?"*

"Coming!" She glances at the door, her eyebrows drawing together.

"You don't have to do this if you don't want to."

Margot gulps, shaking her head. "I do. My reputation is all tied up with Ivy's business now, so I need to clear my name. For her sake."

The actress stands up, brushing her hands down her sides. She smooths her hair down, taking a deep breath as she stares at herself in the mirror. Swinging her gaze to me, she puts her hand to my cheek.

"Thank you, Dante."

"You want me to come out there with you? I can stand where you can see me, and if you ever get nervous, just look at me and remember to breathe."

Margot's shoulders relax, and a soft smile tugs at her lips. "I'd like that."

Nodding, I follow her to the dressing room door. My heart bangs against my ribcage, and I feel a connection with Margot that I've rarely felt with anyone besides my family. She glances over her shoulder at me, and a bolt of lightning passes through my chest.

I may have come here for Luca, but I'm staying for Margot...

...and I know I'm in trouble.

7

MARGOT

When I sit in front of the cameras and feel the heat of the studio lights on my skin, my nerves arc up again. But Dante stands just beside the camera, and the sight of his strong, safe body brings me back down from the edge.

Mel adjusts my hair one last time, staring into my eyes and winking at me. "You'll do great."

I smile, trying to believe her.

I do the interview, saying exactly what Felicity told me to say. I talk about my overdose, my recovery, my anxiety, and all the ways that I've changed over the past months. I focus on the positives, and deflect any unwanted questions.

I don't talk about the baby, or my diagnosis, for obvious reasons. I'm pretty sure Felicity would have a heart attack if I dropped those bombshells without warning her.

Whenever I feel the bundle of nerves in my stomach get tighter, I glance over at the Prince. His eyes stay glued on me and I can sense the waves of calm that he sends my way.

We're connected. It's odd and comforting—and perfect.

After the interview is over, my publicist is beaming as I'm ushered back to the car.

It's not until I'm sitting down next to Dante that I let out a deep sigh, glancing over at him.

"Thank you."

He smiles, putting his arm around my shoulders and pulling me close. "That was impressive," he says.

I just laugh, resting my head on his chest as the car starts moving.

"I mean it," he says. "I don't know if I'd have been able to pull myself together like that and look so poised and humble. You did really well."

"Thank you," I say softly, inhaling his scent.

I'm not one to feel this comfortable with men—or anyone, really—so soon after meeting them. It takes me a long time to open up to people. The only other man I've been sort of close to was Prince Beckett, and that was just a one-night stand after being jealous and fed-up that Luca wasn't interested in me. It wasn't real.

I can't remember the last time I had a boyfriend. It's too hard to trust people when you're in this industry. You never know who is genuine and who just wants to use you for publicity.

But with Dante, it's different. He makes me feel at ease, even when he's seen me at my most vulnerable. He seems to understand me on a level that I didn't even know was possible, and I only met him yesterday.

When we get back to the house, I let out a sigh. Dante helps me out of the car and keeps his hand on my lower back as we make our way inside. When he steps away from me to take his jacket off, I miss his touch and the warmth of his body close to mine. I watch him hang up the jacket and then swing his eyes back to mine.

"You doing okay, Margot?"

I smile. "Yeah. Thanks to you. Don't know how I would have done that if you hadn't been there."

"Well, you've helped my brother out a lot, making it easier for him to be with Ivy. I guess I owe it to you."

I smile to hide the twinge of disappointment that passes through me. Is it wrong that I was hoping he was being nice to me just because he wanted to? Not because of some sense of obligation to his brother?

"I need to do a few things for my brother," he adds. "Will you be okay on your own?"

"I'll be fine," I say, putting a brave smile on. "Thanks again."

Watching the Prince walk away, bitterness coats my mouth. My body is still rattled from my panic attack, and I feel like I need to do something to relax.

Jumping in my car, I ignore the bad feeling at the pit of my stomach when I drive through the mansion gates. I always get this feeling when I go anywhere on my own, but I need to do it today. I need to prove to myself that I'm capable of living a normal life, and not be engulfed by fears of all the bad things that might happen, or the inevitable degeneration of my body.

I have a life to live now. I need to go out and live it.

I drive to my favorite spa, where I know they'll be able to fit me in for a massage or a facial without an appointment.

Hey, I never said there weren't perks to being famous—I just said there are downsides, too.

When I get to the spa, the receptionist smiles at me and leads me to a private room. As soon as the soothing aromas of lemongrass and lavender hit me, a smile drifts over my lips.

I just did the most difficult thing I've had to do in a while. That interview is something I've been dreading for weeks, and Felicity said it went perfectly. Even Prince Dante was impressed.

Now that it's done, I can take some time for myself. Hopefully, it'll take the pressure off Ivy, and we can both just enjoy some down time.

Today's interview was a big deal. Yesterday's opening of the bakery was an even bigger deal. I deserve a little bit of pampering.

My usual massage therapist comes in, and I spend the next hour in and out of blissful, relaxing sleep. She massages my entire body from head to toe, and when she leaves the room to let me get dressed, I just lay there for a few minutes to soak up the last few minutes of relaxation.

I have an eye pillow on, and a sheet covering my body when the door opens again. She must have come back in to finish up the treatment. Did I say I wanted a facial, as well? I can't remember exactly what I ordered.

I wait a few moments, anticipating the soft sound of her voice as she tells me what she's going to do.

Instead, a man clears his throat.

"Well, well, well..." Hunter says. "Margot LeBlanc is back in front of the cameras."

I scramble up, clutching the sheet to my body as the eye pillow falls to the ground.

My ex-agent is standing near the door, running his eyes down my nearly-naked body. A slimy feeling follows his gaze as fear ices my veins. My grip tightens on the sheet as I hold it tight to my body.

"How did you get in here? I'm calling security."

"How quickly things change," Hunter says, shaking his head. His eyes are beady and black. "I've been with you from the very start. I got you your first audition—or have you forgotten?"

"You know what I haven't forgotten? How you somehow sourced live E. coli bacteria and planted it in my sister's bakery, hospitalizing dozens of people. One of whom, by the way, was my pregnant sister. I haven't forgotten *that*."

My hand drifts to my abdomen when I say the word 'pregnant,' and Hunter's eyes follow the movement. His eyebrow arches slightly, and my whole body turns cold. The last thing I want is for Hunter to know that I'm pregnant with Prince Beckett's child.

That's exactly the kind of information he would use against me. I need *less* stress in my life, not more.

"I'm here as a courtesy," Hunter says, flicking his eyes back up to my face. I'm still clutching the sheet to my chest. The aromatherapy scents which were so soothing before now stick to the back of my throat, choking me. I feel naked, exposed, and weak.

"What courtesy is that?" I try to keep my voice steady, but a tremor sneaks into the words. After the interview today and the mess that Dante left in my head, I don't know how much more of this I can take.

"You should distance yourself from your sister and her new boyfriend. Protect yourself."

"From what?"

Hunter just snorts, shaking his head. "I thought you'd appreciate the warning. I've heard rumors about the Prince's half-brother."

"What have you heard?" My voice is strangled, and I gulp past a lump in my throat.

"Nothing concrete."

"Stay away from them." I suck in a labored breath. "And from me. You're not welcome here, Hunter."

My old agent's eyes darken. His mouth twists downward, and a shadow passes over his face. "I came here because I still care about you, Margot. I wanted to warn you so you wouldn't get caught up in anything. But if you do, it's your own fault. I can see that you don't want my help, even after everything I've done for you."

Words stick to my throat as I watch him turn back to the door and step out of the room. I rush to lock it, leaning against the door as I exhale. Dropping my head in my hands, I let out a groan.

It was too much to hope for that Hunter would be out of my life for good. When I found out about his involvement in the bakery contamination, I fired him on the spot. I hoped that would be the end of it.

Sounds like I was wrong.

With trembling hands, I put my clothing back on and exit the massage room. I pay quickly, glancing over my shoulder the whole time. It feels like someone is watching me. The persistent dread in my gut gets stronger, and I hurry to my car.

It's not until I'm back home with the door locked that I finally take a full breath.

8

DANTE

I HEAR the door slam and my ears perk up. I've spent the day mapping out all the security risks that might exist here and talking to Theo on the phone about the progress of the search for Beckett.

Okay—maybe I've done a little bit of thinking about Margot, too. I might have Googled her name once or twice. Sue me.

My mind keeps drifting back to her. To the way she looked at that interview. Beautiful, vulnerable, and brave. She's living her life in a way that I have always been too afraid to do. She suffers from the same anxieties as I do, but she faces them head-on.

There's so much more to her than just the long-haired blonde beauty that's portrayed in the media.

I stand up, closing my laptop and locking it in my brief-case before heading downstairs. Margot is leaning against the door, taking deep breaths.

"Everything okay?"

Margot jumps, glancing up at me. Her face relaxes when she recognizes me, and she finally nods. "Yeah, I'm okay."

"Did something happen?"

Margot licks her lips, and my eyes follow the movement. Even when she looks worried, I can't ignore the effect that she has on my body. Whenever she's near, the room heats up a few degrees.

The actress runs her fingers through her hair, letting out a deep breath and finally forcing a smile onto her lips.

"It's fine. I just ran into my old agent."

"The one who tried to hurt your sister?"

She nods. "Yeah. That one. He told me to stay away from her and Luca. Sounded all evil and ominous." She laughs nervously, but I can sense the tension coming off her in waves.

I close the distance between us, sliding my hands over her hips. Margot's eyes lift up to mine, and her chest caves in as she shakes her head.

"It's been a tough day," she finally says.

I run my fingers over her jaw, feeling the electric heat that flows down my arm as I touch her. Being this close to her makes my head spin. When she slides her tongue out to lick her lips again, all my blood rushes between my legs. I should be worried about the security risk, but with Margot in my arms, all I can think of is her. Margot melts into me, wrapping her arms around my waist. My fingers tangle into her hair, and I rest my face next to hers.

"You okay?" I whisper.

This isn't what I expected. I thought I'd come here and take Luca home. At worst, I'd stay here and stick by his side.

In the past two days, though, I haven't felt the need to see Luca at all. He's a grown man—he can take care of himself.

It's Margot I feel drawn to. She's fragile and vulnerable, and she's facing everything I've hidden away from.

I pull my face away, staring into her eyes.

"I'm sorry," she whispers.

"For what?"

"I don't know. For being so needy."

I would laugh, if the moment wasn't so heavy. She's been the opposite of needy. She's been brave and open. She's done things that I'd never be able to do. To face her fears like she did today, and then go back out and see the man who tried to hurt her family without breaking down... Margot is stronger than she gives herself credit for.

I feel drawn to her in a way that I never expected. Of course, when I look at her deep, blue eyes, her full lips, her perfect nose, I see beauty. But that's not what makes me yearn for her.

It's her spirit. She's unbreakable.

Margot's fingers crawl up my chest, curling into my shirt. Her breath hitches, and I feel her heartbeat speed up. My fingers drift down her neck, pushing her hair over her shoulder and sliding over her collarbone.

Her skin is slightly oily, and it smells like scented massage oils. An image flashes in my mind of Margot, oiled up and splayed on top of a massage bed with my hands rubbing her down.

I groan.

She shivers gently, exhaling as I dip my head toward her. Lifting her chin up, her eyes widen.

I pause. "Is this okay?"

Margot nods. "Yes."

My heart thumps. My hand sinks into her hips as the other drifts back up to her jaw. I run my thumb over her lower lip before finally pressing my mouth to hers.

Margot moans gently as her lips part. She swipes her tongue over mine and I taste the fruity sweetness of her lips. Curling my fingers into the nape of her neck, I pull her closer.

She melts into me, deepening our kiss as her arms wrap around me.

I take a step forward, caging her against the front door. Margot's hips roll toward me, and I groan. Running my hands over her curves makes me want to tear the clothes off her body and take her right here, right now.

It feels too good to have her next to me. I need all of her. I need to taste her skin, her pussy, her kiss. I need to plunge myself deep inside her and make her mine.

She gasps, pinned against the door as I kiss her neck, her ear, her jaw. Her fingernails scrape over my scalp, sending shivers all the way down to my cock. I'm rock hard, and I know she can feel it. She grinds herself against me, moaning gently as our kiss gets messier.

It doesn't matter. There are no cameras here.

Her teeth scrape over my lower lip, nipping at me as she kisses me harder. I grunt, pressing my length into her stomach.

It feels like a volcano erupting without warning. I've spent the last day and a half pushing down the feelings that have been mounting inside me, and now I feel like I could rip this beauty's clothes off and take her right here on the marble floor.

Panting, I pull back. I lean my forehead against hers as we both catch our breath. She rests her head against the door, looking at me through her lashes.

"Whoa."

"Yeah," I say between breaths.

"I wasn't expecting that."

"Me neither." I gulp. "Are you... Are you okay with it?"

Margot smiles, and I think it's the first genuine smile I've seen from her. Not an embarrassed smile, not a polite or forced smile. A real, full grin.

"I'm okay with it." She runs her fingers through the hair on the side of my head. Her touch sends tingles tumbling down my spine. Curling her hands into fists, she pulls my hair gently.

I grunt, smiling. "Your touch feels incredible."

"I was going to say the same thing about yours."

Her eyes are bright and completely clear. Gone is the fear and the haze that clouded them before. She smiles again, and a flame ignites in my chest.

I like this girl more than I'm willing to admit to myself.

A car pulls up outside, and we fall apart. Margot clears her throat, smoothing her hair down.

Ivy and Luca burst through the door, laughing about something. Ivy glances from me to Margot, arching an eyebrow.

Luca does the same and I straighten my shoulders. "Luca, you're home," I say, cringing at the squeakiness in my voice. "I was hoping to go over some security things with you."

"Sure." He grins, glancing at Margot again. "You two just hanging out in the hallway?"

"I just got home," Margot says. "Anyone want some food? I had the chef make some extra meals for the week."

"I'm starving," Ivy says, following her sister into the kitchen.

Luca's still staring at me with a grin plastered on his face. "Well, lead the way. I want to hear all about the *security risks* you've been working on."

I ignore him, gesturing to the stairs. "Let's go to my room."

As we walk by the kitchen, I can't resist stealing one last glance at Margot. She looks up as I walk by, redness flushing over her cheeks when our eyes meet.

A tremor passes through my heart. I'm definitely in big, big trouble.

I lead Luca to my room, where I pull out my laptop.

I run him through everything I've planned so far.

"We'll bring some people we trust over from Argyle. I have half a dozen security staff on a plane already, so they'll be here by tonight. I want to beef up security around the house and the bakery. We should keep Ivy and Margot well-protected, since they might be a target."

Luca nods.

"I've also gotten our best two guys to be your team. Theo insisted that you take the best of the best to keep you safe until Beckett is found."

Luca grunts, shaking his head. "Put them on Ivy."

"What?"

"The best guys. I want them protecting Ivy."

"Luca..."

He holds up a hand, silencing me. I stare at my older brother, once again hit by the realization that he isn't the impulsive young man I once knew. He's grown into something stronger.

"We need to draw Beckett out, and I refuse to live in fear of what he might do. The best way to get Beckett to make a mistake is to dangle the best bait possible in front of him." Luca's eyes stay trained on mine. "And the best bait is me."

"Luca, I'm not going to use you..."

"It's not up to you," he interrupts. "I want the extra staff on Ivy, Margot, and the bakery. We'll keep one guy undercover on me. I'm going to start making more public appearances. Being more visible."

"More vulnerable, you mean."

Luca nods. "It's the only way to end this."

"It's not the only way, Luca."

"Well, it's the quickest way."

I take a deep breath, roughing a hand through my hair. "Okay, well, I'll be by your side."

Luca tilts his head. "Dante, I'm not sure you understand. I'm going to be calling reporters, getting them to show up wherever I go. My face will be plastered on every website, every newspaper, every tabloid there is. I'm going to make myself so visible that Beckett won't be able to resist coming out of the woodwork."

"I understand completely."

"You've spent the last couple of decades hiding your face, Dante," Luca says, drawing his brows together. "Why would you give that up?"

I take a deep breath, glancing at my laptop screen. I close it, knowing I'll have to re-work our entire security plan. Dragging my gaze back up to my brother, I shrug.

"I've spent my whole life living in fear of what people might say about me. It's been a good life, but I've let my fears stop me."

I think of Margot, and how she put on a brave face minutes after recovering from her panic attack. She stepped out in front of the cameras and gave the performance of a lifetime. Would I have been able to do that?

I'm not sure.

"You need me, Luca. Whether you want to admit it or not." I look at my brother, shaking my head. "If this is how you want to play it to draw Beckett out, I'm not going to let you do it on your own."

Luca's lips stretch into a grin. "The reclusive prince is coming out of hiding."

I blow the air out of my lungs, shaking my head. "I guess I am."

I grunt when Luca's body slams into mine. I wrap my

arms around him to return the hug, feeling a flush of affection for my brother. Luca pulls away, his eyes misting.

"I know that this is a big deal to you, Dante."

"You're my brother," I answer simply. "I wasn't there for you when you broke your back. I let you push me away—I'm not going to let it happen again."

Luca squeezes my shoulder with his meaty hand, nodding. "Thank you."

I watch him walk away, and I know he's going to see Ivy. My feet are itching to take me to Margot, but I resist. I know that part of the reason it's been so easy for me to stay here—so easy for me to decide to step into the spotlight—is because of her.

Margot has started unravelling something inside me, and I don't know what will happen when it comes undone.

9

IVY

MARGOT IS FLUSHED. I tilt my head, staring at my sister. She doesn't meet my gaze.

"What's going on with you?"

Margot arches an eyebrow and shrugs. "Nothing. Why?"

"You seem different. Flustered."

"I'm fine."

My sister grabs a piece of banana bread that I've brought back from the bakery and takes a big bite out of it. I try not to let the surprise register on my face. I'm still not used to seeing her eat a regular amount of food.

Maybe it's the pregnancy that's making her look like this.

"How have you been feeling?" I nod to her abdomen.

Margot slides her hand over her stomach and lets out a sigh. "Stressed."

"It'll be okay."

"Easy for you to say, with your royal boyfriend who loves you more than anything." Margot chuckles bitterly. "What have I got? A flagging career and an unplanned baby."

"The same was true for me a couple of weeks ago, Margot. Now look!"

My sister smiles sadly. I know she doesn't believe that things will work out. She's worried about what the media will say about her pregnancy, since people will surely do the math and find out she either got pregnant at her retreat or shortly before. News of her overdose was highly publicized, and things have only gotten more dramatic since then.

I reach for a piece of banana bread of my own, taking a bite as I think.

"You still don't want to tell me who the father is?"

Margot shakes her head.

"But...you know who it is?"

My sister's eyes snap up to mine. They flash as she swallows the bite of banana bread in her mouth. "Yes, I know who the father is."

"Why don't you want to tell me? I can help you, Margot."

She smiles sadly, shaking her head. "You can't. It doesn't matter, anyway. It's better if you don't know."

"But, why?"

Instead of answering, Margot just wraps her arms around me. She squeezes me tight, and then pulls away to look in my eyes. "I'm just glad we're on good terms again."

"You're my sister. We're always going to be close. Until we're old biddies wearing matching pantsuits and pearls, complaining about kids these days."

A shadow crosses Margot's face, and she nods. "Yeah. I hope so."

"We have a doctor's appointment tomorrow morning. You still good to go?"

We've been scheduling our OB-GYN appointments at the same time to help cover up her pregnancy from the media. My pregnancy is public, so if anyone sees us, it looks like she's just accompanying me to my appointments.

"I'll be ready." Margot gives me a sad smile and then

walks out of the kitchen. I hear her soft footsteps walking up the stairs, and I let my shoulders drop.

I'm worried about her. She's isolating herself from everyone she knows except for me, Luca, and her hair stylist. She barely talks to her publicist anymore, and she used to be fully involved in her public image and her career. Ever since Hunter revealed that he was behind the E. coli contamination, I think Margot has felt like she can't trust anyone.

I can't blame her.

Lifting my eyes when Luca walks into the kitchen, I let a smile drift over my lips. He wraps his arms around me and nuzzles his nose against mine. Melting into his arms, I let myself be comforted by his touch.

I love this man more than life itself. When he runs his hand over my stomach, I know I'm the luckiest woman in the world.

Luca presses his lips to mine. "I love you, Ivy."

"Love you too, Your Highness."

He grins at the formal title, kissing the tip of my nose.

"What did Dante want?" I ask.

"He put together a security plan. He doesn't want you alone at the bakery anymore—thinks it's a weak spot for someone to get to me through you."

I frown. "Okay. Makes sense."

"He's bringing a few trusted security personnel over from Argyle. We'll beef up security here and at the bakery, and make sure that you and Margot are never alone."

"And what about you?"

"I'll be fine."

"What's that supposed to mean?" I stare into Luca's eyes, trying to find the meaning behind his words. His face looks shuttered, as if he's trying to hide something from me. "Tell me," I say.

Luca exhales, shaking his head. "The less you know, the better."

"Incorrect," I snap. "My sister won't tell me who the father of her child is, I'm being followed by bodyguards everywhere, and now you're telling me that you won't even tell me what you're planning? Someone tried to kill you, Luca. Another man tried to sabotage my bakery and my reputation. I have a right to know."

My heart squeezes. Luca is the love of my life. I know it in the depths of my soul, and nothing can take any certainty away from me. I know that I belong with him, and that means taking the good with the bad.

That means we have to be completely honest with each other about everything.

Curling my fingers around his neck, I try to read his face. "Luca, we're in this together. It's not just about you anymore, and you can't just isolate yourself. There's me and the baby to think about. I need to know what's going on. We're a team."

Luca closes his eyes, leaning his forehead against mine. "It's hard to change the way I think. I've been on my own for so long."

"You've pushed people away your whole life, but I'm not going to let you do that to me."

Luca smiles and nods as he relents. "Fine. But promise you won't get mad."

"I'm not promising anything."

He groans, finally pulling away to lean against the kitchen counter. Roughing a hand through his hair, Luca chews his lip as he tries to find the right words.

"We're keeping security to a minimum on me to bait Beckett. I want this place and the bakery to be Fort Knox, but I'll be exposed."

"Luca..." Fear ices my spine. "Have you forgotten that you're going to be a father?"

"That's exactly why I'm doing this, Ivy. I need to protect you from Beckett, and the easiest way to do that is to draw him out of whatever hole he's hiding in."

"I don't like it."

"That's why I didn't want to tell you."

"Do you know if Beckett is in Farcliff?"

Luca shakes his head. "No idea. But I'll probably be making some more trips to the castle and making public appearances to tempt him to come out. Dante said he'd do it, too."

"Dante, the brother who has lived a hermit life? He wants to be out in public? I thought you said he hasn't had his picture taken in over a decade."

"He hasn't," Luca responds. "And I also said he's one of the best people I've ever met. He said pretty much the same thing you just did—that he won't let me push him away. He's going to be with me, doing public appearances and trying to get Beckett to make a mistake."

I sigh, staring over Luca's shoulder into nothing. The love of my life and father of my child is deliberately putting himself on display to try to end this threat looming over us. It makes my chest swell with pride and my stomach twist in knots all at once.

"What about Hunter?" I ask, turning to look at Luca. "Are we going to do anything about him? Do you think he's dangerous?"

"I'll talk to Margot."

Luca wraps his arms around me and I melt into his embrace. I rest my head on his broad shoulder, listening to the beating of his heart. It thumps against me, calming me down with every beat.

The Prince strokes my head, laying a gentle kiss in my hair.

"I'm doing this for you and the baby, Ivy," he whispers. "When that baby comes, I don't want there to be any danger. We have to end this before he's born."

"He?"

Luca looks down at me as I arch an eyebrow. He grins, shrugging. "I think it's a boy."

"Men always say that," I laugh, shaking my head. "But as soon as a little girl comes out, your heart melts and you turn into a gooey mess."

"Who are you calling a gooey mess?"

The Prince squeezes me tight, picking me up to place me on the kitchen counter. He crushes his lips against mine as my heart flips inside my chest.

Every kiss feels like the first time. Every touch sends sparks flying over my skin. Every gaze makes my stomach clench and my thighs squeeze together.

I love this man with all my heart.

I just hope he's right about Beckett, and that this will be over before the baby comes.

10

MARGOT

NOW THAT HUNTER is gone from my life, I'm realizing what a toxic influence he was. He'd constantly be in my ear, criticizing Ivy. He'd tell me that my sister was a leech, that she didn't care about me, that she was only using me for my money and to have a place to live.

He used to say that Melissa was another social climber, and she couldn't be trusted. The only person I could trust was him.

That's why he was always the one I would call when I had a problem. The one who saved me from parties and paraded me around for the paparazzi. The one who held the keys to every job I ever landed. He was the one that was using me. I see that now.

Taking care of my mental and physical health and finding out I'm pregnant has transformed my life in ways I could never have imagined. My priorities have completely shifted from myself and my career, to taking care of my baby. I was in such a haze of alcohol and bitterness that I didn't see what was right in front of me.

Ivy is the only person that has ever cared about me. She's the only one that truly wants me to be well.

Not successful. Not famous. Not rich.

She wants me to be healthy, happy, and *well.*

I take a deep breath, smoothing my hair down as I stare at myself in the mirror. I'm getting ready for my doctor's appointment after another night of fitful sleep. Huntington's disease has always loomed over us. When Ivy got her results, she ripped them open right then and there, letting out a happy sigh when she saw that she was negative.

I wasn't so lucky. It took me months to work up the courage just to read the results.

Now, I know. My body will break down just as my mother's did. My child will have to watch me die in the same way I had to watch Mama fall apart.

Turning away from the mirror, I try to push the thought out of my mind. The gremlins in my mind cackle, letting words echo in my mind.

What if the baby gets it, too?

I ball my hands into fists and force myself to go downstairs and into the waiting car.

My sister smiles at me as the driver takes us to our doctor's appointments. I glance behind us, trying to spot any paparazzi that may be following.

I haven't even told Felicity that I'm pregnant. She'll blow a gasket when she finds out.

But it doesn't matter, because I have Ivy's support. She hooks her arm into mine and leads me inside the building.

I'm led into the doctor's office and told to sit down. I fidget, bouncing my knee up and down until the doctor walks in. She's wearing a white lab coat and black-framed glasses. After an ultrasound and a few other checks, the doctor smiles at me.

"Everything looks good. All signs point to a healthy baby in there, Ms. LeBlanc."

"Are you sure?"

"As far as we can tell, yes. Now, you have a decision to make. Do you want to get genetic testing done on your baby? It's about time we got on with it, if you want to."

Fear pierces through me. She could do the test now. In a few days, I could find out if my baby has my disease.

I gulp. "I don't know."

The doctor spins to face me, folding her hands on her lap. "It's a difficult decision. I understand that. As I explained last time, usually we only do the testing if you know you'll terminate if it's positive. If you don't get the test, your child will have to decide for themselves if they want to be tested once they turn eighteen."

Don't you love when people who couldn't possibly understand say, 'I understand'?

Being faced with the certainty that my baby will carry my disease would leave me with a horrible choice. Do I condemn it to a short, painful lifetime as the baby's body breaks down, or do I end its life before it even starts?

I shake my head. I would never be able to terminate. This baby is more a part of me than I could have ever imagined, and I can't bear the thought of losing it.

I know that other people would make that choice, and it might be a mercy for the child. But this baby has saved me from my own self-destruction. This baby is everything to me.

I shake my head to hide the tears in my eyes. "I don't want the test."

"Margot," she says softly. "There's a fifty percent chance..."

"I know. I can't. I want to have this baby."

The doctor nods. "Okay."

And that's the end of it.

Guilt snakes in my veins, squeezing me from the inside out. For the millionth time, I rake myself over the coals for my choices.

My baby was conceived with a bad man, in a haze of substance abuse. They said I had heroin in my system. Heroin! The most I've ever done was a bit of acid at a music festival a few years ago. I don't...

I squeeze my eyes shut, not wanting to think about it.

How is it possible that everything looks healthy? How is it possible that everything would turn out okay? Am I making the wrong choice?

The way I feel is almost like survivor's guilt. I couldn't possibly come out of this unscathed. Why do *I* get to be so lucky?

I let out a breath, squeezing my eyes shut. I almost don't believe the doctor. I've spent the last four months worried about the damage I might have done to my baby. Ever since I've found out about the pregnancy, I've been doing everything right. Before that, though...

I shake my head, not wanting to think about my life before the retreat. I was spiraling out of control. I was stuck in my own head.

Maybe I *did* willingly do heroin. I don't remember much from that night except taking Beckett up to my bedroom. I was on a self-destructive war path.

The doctor sighs, taking a seat beside me. She takes my hand in hers and stares at me with soft, kind eyes.

"As far as we can tell, your baby is completely normal. I know this pregnancy might not have come at the ideal time for you, but try not to stress out about it too much. You're going to be a loving, wonderful mother."

A sob racks through my throat, surprising me. Emotion

chokes me, and I shake my head. "I don't know about that. I've been so irresponsible."

"You've done everything right from the moment you found out you were pregnant. You've completely changed your life. You should be proud of yourself. You're exactly the type of person that the rest of us should look up to."

I'd laugh if I wasn't afraid it would turn into an ugly sob.

The doctor's kind words bounce off me and fall to the ground. I let them slide away, not believing any of it.

I'm the furthest thing from an inspiration. People keep telling me that I'm a role model and that I'm brave and strong. Felicity told me that the feedback on my interview has been overwhelmingly positive.

She said I'm 'back in the game.'

What game, exactly? Why does it feel like I'm always losing?

The only thing I have is persistent, nagging anxiety about my entire world crashing down around me.

The doctor gives me one last smile and then leaves the room. When I rejoin Ivy, she's beaming.

"Good news?" I ask, forcing a smile.

"I'm having twins!" Ivy laughs, clapping her hands over her mouth before throwing them around me. She hugs me tight. "I'm so glad we're doing this together, Margot. It would be scary on my own."

"You've got Luca, too," I remind her.

Ivy's face softens, and a smile stretches across her lips. "Yeah," she says. "I do."

WE HEAD BACK to *Spoonful of Sugar* together. Ivy's friends, the twins Giselle and Georgina, are working behind the counter.

They follow us into the back of the bakery, looking at Ivy

expectantly. Ivy gives them both a kiss, mumbling something to them. The twins squeal, hugging her.

"Twins!" Giselle exclaims. At least, I think it's Giselle. One of them has a mole on her left cheek, but I can't quite remember which is which. They both change their hair color so often it's hard to keep up.

"Lucky," Georgina says, wrapping Ivy in another hug.

I smile, sliding my own hand over my stomach. As the dread inside me melts away, I allow myself to be happy for just a moment.

I'm pregnant with a healthy baby. My recovery is going strong, and Hunter is out of my life. Ivy and I are closer than ever, and my baby will have not one, but two cousins to play with their entire lives.

A warm, comforting hand slides over my lower back, and I turn to see Prince Dante beside me. He smiles and I lean into him, feeling my heart tug in his direction.

I have him, too. Not that he and I are anything. We've only known each other for a matter of days. But at least for a little while, I can enjoy his attention, his affection, and his kisses, can't I?

He fills my heart up to the brim, and that can't be a bad thing.

"How was the doctor?" Dante asks, nodding to Ivy.

"It was good. Everything's healthy and normal," I say. "Ivy's having twins."

Dante's face breaks into a smile—a real, genuine smile—and my heart melts into a puddle of goo in the middle of my chest.

"You like kids?" I ask, my voice squeaking. He still doesn't know I'm pregnant, but seeing his face light up like this makes me want to tell him.

"Love them," he says. "Almost as much as animals. They're the only two honest creatures on this earth."

"I'll agree with you there," I smile.

He excuses himself and moves to congratulate Ivy. She beams at him, glancing over his shoulder to see Luca stepping into the bakery. My sister's face brightens so much when she sees Prince Luca that I can't help but feel happy for her.

Dante smiles at Ivy, too, and I have such a strong urge to tell him about my baby. I want to see that look on his face when he looks at me, too.

But it wouldn't be the same. Ivy is his brother's partner, so he can be happy for her like a brother.

What am I?

The girl he kissed yesterday. The famous actress that he lives with. His flame of the month.

If I tell him I'm pregnant, I might lose his attention and his affection, and I'm not sure I want to do that. Dante's eyes swing back to me, and a shiver of heat runs down my spine.

No, I'm not ready to let go of whatever is going on between us. The way he looks at me makes me feel alive again. There are so few good things in my life right now, so few things that make me feel like everything is going to be okay...

...I don't want to lose what little joy I have.

I'll tell him I'm pregnant, just not right now.

Ivy, the twins, and Luca head back out front to help the bakery's customers, and Dante grins at me.

"Looks like we're alone again."

11

DANTE

Is it just me, or do Margot's boobs look especially juicy right now? It takes all my self-control not to throw her over my shoulder and drag her back to the house.

Every hour that goes by with Margot in my presence, I want her more. Seconds tick by like the beats of my heart, and my body tenses up in anticipation.

Her chest rises and falls with every breath, and I sweep my eyes over her perfect curves. My whole body thrums, and I wonder who exactly I've become.

I'm not the type of guy who has near-uncontrollable urges around women. I'm not the kind of guy who welcomes the attention of the media, or volunteers to go on a press tour with my brother. I've spent the last couple of decades of my life avoiding those things completely.

Now, I'm ready to throw my privacy out the window.

I can tell myself that it's for Luca. I can pretend that I'm doing this to protect my brother.

The truth is, I want to do anything I can to stay here. I feel drawn to Margot in a way that I never even imagined. As my eyes drift up to her lush, pink lips, the thought of kissing her screams through my head. I can't think of anything else except tasting her lips again.

Leaning toward Margot, my breath catches. I don't even care that anyone could walk in on us. I don't care that Luca and Ivy might see. By the way her fingers curl into my shirt, and her head tilts toward me, I know that she wants me too.

Ever since our kiss last night, I haven't been able to get her out of my head. One hit of her, and I'm already addicted.

I need more.

Margot lets out a soft sigh, shaking her head. "What are you doing to me?"

"Whatever you want me to," I growl.

Redness blossoms over her cheeks, and she glances at me through her eyelashes. Sucking her lip between her teeth, she presses her chest against mine. My cock throbs, always hypersensitive whenever Margot is near.

I'm ready to slam her against the wall and plunge myself inside her. Right here. Health code violations be damned. I'll spread her legs here in her sister's bakery.

Before I can do that, though, Ivy pokes her head through the door. "Media caught wind of Luca being here. Huge rush. I need you to pull some cupcakes and Danishes out for me."

Margot jumps away from me, nodding to her sister. She glances at me quickly before ducking into the walk-in fridge. Coming out with a big tray of pastries, she gives me the slightest, sexiest smile I've ever seen from her.

There's a playful side to Margot that I haven't gotten to know yet. We've been so consumed by worry and security issues that I haven't had a chance to see what she's like when life isn't upside down. I know there's another side to her, though. I can see it in her eyes.

I just hope I have the chance to get to know it.

She carries the tray out to the front of the bakery, and I

follow her out with another. As soon as we step out into the main cafe area, phones and cameras are trained on Margot. She puts the tray of baked goods down and smiles at the assembled crowd, reaching over to sign some autographs.

I shrink away, dropping the fresh pastries on the counter and heading back to the safety of the kitchen. I glance through the little round window at Margot as she plasters a smile on her face.

I'm starting to get to know her smiles. There's the polite smile that she uses for fans and interviews. That's the smile I see most. There's the sad smile that I see second most often. Sometimes it turns into a bitter grimace, and sometimes it fades away completely.

Only once or twice have I seen her really smile.

It makes me want to climb into her brain and clean all the cobwebs away. I want to know why she's troubled, and carry those burdens for her. I want her to laugh and smile genuinely all the time.

Most importantly, I want her to do those things *with me*. By my side. Always.

I watch her take selfies with fans, sign autographs, and just be the celebrity that she's always been. She acts with grace and professionalism, but I can see in the curve of her shoulders that she's tired.

Meanwhile, I stare through the window in the door as my heart races, afraid to step back out in case a camera flashes in my face.

Like a coward.

How can she be so comfortable with so many people clamoring for her attention? How can she smile as dozens of cameras are pointed at her? How does she not feel like a caged animal?

Turning away from the window, I lean against the bakery

wall. For the first time since I spoke to Luca last night, I'm seriously regretting my decision to go out in public with him. I don't know if I can handle that kind of attention. Doing what Margot is doing right now is my personal idea of hell.

The door swings open and Margot appears, letting out a deep breath as she puts a hand to her forehead.

"That was intense," she sighs.

"How do you do it?"

Margot glances at me, arching an eyebrow. "Do what?"

"Deal with that many people screaming for you. It wasn't even that many—maybe a couple of dozen? The thought of being out there, in front of that many people and that many cameras...it makes me want to throw up."

Margot flashes a smile at me. A real one. "You want to know the truth?"

I nod.

"Makes me want to throw up, too."

I laugh, shaking my head. "Somehow I don't really believe that."

She shrugs, turning away from me. "You don't have to believe me for it to be the truth. Lots of people think lots of things about me that have nothing to do with the truth."

Once again, I realize I don't know Margot LeBlanc at all. I have an image of her in my head, a vision of who she is and what she wants—but I don't know what she really thinks.

The only thing I know for sure is that there's a lot more to her than meets the eye.

"Can you give me a hand with the trays? Ivy needs more salted caramel cupcakes already." Margot nods to the walk-in fridge.

I follow her in, trying not to stare at the sway of her ass. She points to one of the trays, reaching for the edge.

"Lots of people think I love public appearances just

because I'm good at them. I've been doing this since I was twelve years old, Your Highness," Margot says, glancing at me. "Doesn't mean I enjoy it."

"So, why do you do it?"

Margot shrugs. "It's my job."

"You could always walk away from it if you don't like it. I did."

Her shoulders drop, and I take a step closer to her. Gently, with my hand on her hip, I turn her to face me. She drags her eyes up to mine and I watch her blink mist out of her eyes, shaking her head as she takes a deep breath.

"I'm fine," she says, wiping her eyes. "There's just a lot going on right now."

I can't resist any longer. I slide my hand over her jaw and cup her cheek, bringing my lips to hers. I don't want to kiss her like I did last night—all wild and rough. I want to cherish her. Adore her. Worship her.

Margot is strong, yet fragile. She's complicated and intelligent, and she doesn't get enough credit. She faces all the things that I've shied away from with her shoulders thrown back and a smile on her face.

She makes me realize how lucky I truly am to have had the privacy I've enjoyed.

I part my lips, needing to taste her mouth. Swiping my tongue over her lower lip, I groan. How is it possible for one woman to taste so good?

Margot's hands sink into my shoulders, pulling me closer. She moans, tangling her fingers into the hair at the nape of my neck as her body melts into mine. Her chest presses against mine, and I feel her hardened nipples through her shirt.

My hand drifts to her breast. I need to have it in my hand. I need to brush my thumb over her pebbled nipple, and I need to feel her body against mine. I run my hands down her sides, cupping her ass and pulling her closer.

Margot grinds her hips into me, moaning as our kiss gets messier. My lips miss hers and I kiss her jaw, her lower lip. I nip at her, tasting her again as she kisses me harder. Our hot breath sends small clouds dissipating into the cold fridge, but I don't feel anything except the heat of Margot's body.

Fire ignites in my veins, and my shaft hardens to steel.

I want to be inside her.

I *need* to be inside her.

There's never been a woman so surprising, so beautiful, so fucking perfect in her imperfections, and she's the woman for me.

12

MARGOT

As soon as the Prince's lips touch mine, all my hesitations dissolve into nothing.

He's Beckett's brother? Doesn't matter.

He doesn't know I'm pregnant? Irrelevant.

I have an incurable illness that will ravage my body over the next couple of decades? Inconsequential.

I only met him two days ago, and I know we'll never really be together? Beside the point.

Dante's lips are soft, and his touch is possessive. He drops his hand between my legs, and my panties are immediately drenched. As he touches me through the fabric of my pants, a moan slips through my lips.

"Anyone could walk in," I breathe, clawing him closer. I kiss his lips, his jaw, his neck.

"Let them."

Prince Dante slips his hand under my shirt. The heat of his palm against my skin sends sparks shooting through my veins. Heat blooms in the pit of my stomach, teasing the edges of my womb.

My heart thumps.

This is exactly the out-of-control feeling that I've been trying to avoid. Being with Dante is a high. It's a clear and bright high that makes me feel incredible—but it's a high nonetheless. He's a drug.

When he runs his hands up my sides and cups my breast, the protests in my head melt away.

Just because I've been having issues doesn't mean I need to deny myself every pleasure that exists. I won't go into a tailspin just because I kiss a man.

Is this just a kiss, though? It feels like so much more than that.

Dante drops his head to my neck, leaving a trail of kisses down to my collarbone. His breath makes goosebumps blossom on my skin, sending more heat diving toward my center.

I don't protest when he unbuttons my jeans. I don't stop him when he slips his hand between my legs.

I want him. Badly.

Angling my hips toward him, I let out a sigh as his fingers slide against my wetness. He grunts, staring into my eyes. There are no words anymore. We don't need them. A look, a sound, a touch—that's more than enough to say what we feel.

With my eyes, I tell him I want more. With the rocking of my hips, I tell him his hand feels like magic. With a soft moan, I tell him that I never want him to stop.

Dante emits electricity from the tips of his fingers. Everywhere he touches comes alive, and I come apart.

My hands claw at the shelves behind me, knocking a few pastries to the ground. We ignore them. They don't matter. Nothing matters except the Prince's hand between my legs. He kisses my neck, my ear, my jaw, my lips. He slips his fingers inside my opening, earning a gasp from me.

I wrap my arms around him, closing my eyes.

When was the last time a man touched me like this? I can't remember.

The way the Prince touches me is almost reverent. He's not asking for me to touch him in return. He's not wanting anything from me.

He's giving.

I can see it in the way his eyes soften, and how his lips curl into a smile when I moan. My fingers sink into his arms, and he moves those magic fingers to dance over my clit.

The last of my anxieties evaporates as pleasure crests inside me. In that moment, the Prince smashes through the walls I've built inside myself. He blasts through them as if they've never even existed, pushing away every thought in my mind.

There are no worries, no insecurities, no fears.

I'm free.

Every touch of Dante's makes my mind clearer. Every kiss brings me higher.

My thoughts, once cloudy and uncertain, are completely crystalline. It's like the shackles that I've built inside my head are all unlatched at once. The Prince had the key, and he frees me from myself.

I give myself over to the desire coursing through my veins. I let my body do what I haven't been able to do in years.

I come.

It's a symphony of pleasure in my body. A chorus of ecstasy exploding in my veins, catapulting me out of the depths of my own mind into blissful serenity. The Prince moans, crushing his lips to mine as my orgasm rocks through my body.

I tremble against him, clinging onto his shoulders and grasping at his muscles. My legs quake, unable to hold my own weight. My chest heaves as I gulp down breath, after breath, after breath.

The Prince kisses me gently, staring into my eyes. "I've wanted to do that since the moment I saw you," he says, his voice low and gravelly.

My heart skips a beat. I don't remember the last time a man did something like that to me without wanting anything in return.

I search his eyes, looking for some hint of expectation in them. Does he expect me to get on my knees now?

But the only thing I see in Dante's face is affection. He tucks a strand of hair behind my ear and jerks his chin toward the door.

"We should probably bring those cupcakes out now."

A blush stains my cheeks and a giggle slips through my lips.

"Probably, yeah."

Glancing around the walk-in fridge, I survey the damage around us. Half a dozen pastries have fallen off the racks onto the floor. I lick icing off my finger where I accidentally stuck my hand in a cupcake.

The Prince grins, arching an eyebrow. "Stop doing that now, or else I might not let you leave this fridge for another little while."

I grin, biting my lip. "I wouldn't mind that."

Dante leans over and presses another kiss to my lips. Little puffs of electricity sizzle through my body, reminding me of the pleasure he just delivered. The Prince slides his fingers along my jaw and another tingle of energy courses down to my stomach. I lean into him, relishing the intimacy of his touch.

He doesn't know me, yet he understands every part of me.

When the Prince pulls away, I lift my eyes up to his. "Can I tell you a secret?"

"I'd be honored."

"I haven't had an orgasm in three years, give or take a few months."

Prince Dante stares at me. He blinks two or three times, his eyebrows tugging toward each other. "You what?"

I blush. "That's the first time I've come in three years."

"Are you being serious right now?"

"Completely."

He sweeps the back of his fingers over my cheek. "Why not?"

My heart tugs, leaning into his gentle touch. I shrug. "I think it was a mental block. Maybe I just felt like I didn't deserve it."

The Prince shakes his head. "You deserve so much more. If I'd known you hadn't come in three years, I wouldn't have fingered you in a walk-in fridge. I'd have done something a bit more romantic."

I smile, blushing as I shake my head. "It was perfect."

The Prince presses his lips to mine. He wraps his arms around my waist, holding me close to him. I moan, giving myself over to his embrace.

If it feels so right to be in his arms, how could it possibly be wrong?

Dante pulls away and nods to the tray of cupcakes. I smile, helping him unload one from the tall, stainless steel racks holding the trays. When we walk out into the warmth of the bakery, I let out a sigh.

If this is going to continue between us—and I definitely want it to—I have to tell him I'm pregnant. Not only that, I have to tell him that Beckett is the father.

Anything else would be insincere.

Dante glances over his shoulder and flashes a brilliant smile at me. I smile back, but in my heart, I know that my pregnancy will change everything.

Maybe that orgasm in the walk-in fridge is as good as it gets for me. Maybe I've been right all along, and I don't deserve anything more romantic than that.

I shake the thought away, focusing on the tiny jolts of pleasure that still tickle my veins.

Even if the pregnancy changes what's going on between Dante and me, I've still been able to experience something that I thought was completely out of reach. He's still shown me a side of myself that I thought was long gone.

The calm, anxiety-free side. The carefree, orgasmic side. The brave side.

Maybe, now that I know I still have it in me, I'll be able to bring myself to orgasm—even if Prince Dante doesn't want me and my baby.

But even as the thought crosses my mind, I know that it'll never be the same as it is with him.

13

DANTE

THE NEXT WEEK is spent organizing security and making sure all our systems are in order. Luca stays true to his word and has reporters following him everywhere. His face is on every tabloid in Farcliff.

I don't quite succeed in being by his side. I still shy away from the cameras, but my name still shows up in a few headlines.

I hate it.

Every second of it. Every mention of my name. Every sliver of a photograph where I appear.

It makes my gut churn to see my name in big, bold letters.

It's hard to change after so many years of living my life in complete privacy. When cameras flash in my face, I feel like I should be in a zoo. The paparazzi yell at us, asking all kinds of questions designed to get a reaction. Luca handles it with grace, and I just end up seething beside him.

I'm just not cut out for it.

I don't know how Margot does it. How any of them do it.

But I try. I do my best to go with Luca when he's in public, and be another set of eyes and ears as we work on drawing

Beckett out of whatever hole he's hiding in. We both know it'll take time, and all we can do is try to taunt Beckett enough to reveal himself.

As the days pass, I can sense cracks in Luca's facade. Lines appear near his eyes, and his shoulders stoop more than before.

He wants this all to be over. I see him with Ivy, in the evenings, snuggling on the couch. They talk about the bakery, about getting their own place, about giving back to charity.

They talk about the baby and their plans for the future.

They're planning a life together, and I can sense that this whole Beckett threat is holding them back. So, I suck up my discomfort and I go with Luca where he needs to go. We head to bars, restaurants, cafes—anywhere public where we might be photographed.

By the end of the week, I'm exhausted.

Margot seems to pull away from me slightly, putting up walls that she'd let down when I first arrived. She has public appearances of her own, and I don't see much of her. Every chance I get, though, I kiss her. Anytime we're alone together, she seems to melt into my embrace and drop the walls that go up when other people are around.

Two weeks to the day after I arrive in Farcliff, a royal invitation arrives at our doorstep.

Luca waves it toward me, grinning. "Looks like our little media campaign has worked. The Farcliff royal family has caught wind of you being in Farcliff, and we're all invited up to the castle. Me, you, Ivy, and Margot."

I suck a breath in, nodding. "I'm assuming you want to make a big deal out of this? Cameras, reporters, paparazzi?"

Luca tilts his head from side to side. "Ivy and Margot will be there. I'd rather keep it simple."

I try not to look as relieved as I feel. I keep my face still, but Luca still laughs.

"You can pull back from the spotlight, if you want. You've been doing well this week. I appreciate it. I don't need you in the spotlight. Why don't you run things from home?"

I shake my head. "I'm not going to let you do this on your own. Who knows what Beckett might try?"

"Who knows if he'll try anything at all?" Luca asks, shaking his head. "The more time goes on, the more this seems futile. He was a coward to try to poison me. Why would he make some brash attack against me again? He's probably just wallowing somewhere, hating me from afar."

"Maybe, but it's like you said—the best way to get him out in the open is to taunt him."

Luca sighs. "I don't know if it's enough. What set him off last time was my fake relationship with Margot, and then meeting Ivy. I think it made him remember Cara, and how he felt about her. Seeing me alone with you in public might not tempt him to try something stupid."

"Let's just go to the castle, and then reassess. You still want to stay in Farcliff?"

"This is Ivy's home—and mine, too. I've been away from Argyle so long, I'm not sure it's where I want to end up. There's nothing for me there."

I give him a sad smile.

I'm homesick. I'd like nothing more than to pick up and bring him, Ivy, and Margot back to Argyle. Farcliff is sandwiched between the United States and Canada, and it's far too cold up here. I miss the Caribbean warmth of Argyle. The white, sandy beaches and the swaying palm trees. The azure waters, and the laid-back attitude.

I can't even imagine what the real winter will be like here. I've only seen snow twice in my life.

Luca clears his throat, drawing me out of my own head. "You don't have to stay," he says, staring into my eyes.

I shake my head. "You're wrong. I do."

MARGOT LOOKS ABSOLUTELY stunning when we go to Farcliff Castle. Her long, blonde hair is curled in soft waves. Her makeup is flawless. Her body looks unreal. She's wearing a demure, high-neck dress that makes me want to rip it off her gorgeous curves.

I've said it before and I'll say it again—that woman could wear absolutely anything, and she'd look like sex on legs.

She gives me a shy smile as a valet opens the car door for us. He helps her out of the car, and a stab of jealousy stings my heart when the valet's hand touches Margot's. I brush it off, knowing it's ridiculous for me to feel that way.

I've known the woman two weeks, and I'm ready to tear the head off any man who looks at her. At this rate, I'll be decapitating all of Farcliff.

The four of us are led inside the castle, and I take a deep breath.

I've spent my entire life surrounded by this kind of luxury. Ornate rooms, expensive paintings, flawless décor, and an army of staff to keep it all looking perfect.

In a way, it feels good to be in a castle again, but a part of me has enjoyed living at the LeBlanc house. It's just as safe and private as the castle, but it's not nearly as formal. There isn't staff waiting around every corner.

Even though I've spent more time in public, I've felt like I have more privacy in the LeBlanc mansion than I did in Argyle.

Coming to Farcliff Castle makes me feel exposed and nostalgic at the same time.

The four of us stand when King Charlie and his Queen, Elle, walk into the room. I bow for the monarchs, straightening myself up to see King Charlie smiling wide. His three children trail behind, greeting us with bows and curtseys.

Queen Elle is as tall as I am. She puts her hand around her eldest's shoulders, pulling him close. The movement is intimate, and not something I'm used to seeing from royalty. The affection between the kids and the parents is so obvious, it makes my heart squeeze.

I never thought I wanted kids, but seeing the King and Queen of Farcliff with their young ones, and seeing Luca excited over the twins makes me reconsider. Being a father seems like the best thing I could ever do with my life.

Stealing a glance at Margot, I feel my pulse quicken.

The King asks us to sit, and we fall into polite conversation.

Queen Elle looks at me, tilting her head. "I must admit, Prince Dante, I'd never even seen a photo of you before last week."

"That's by design," I smile. "I'm a very private person."

"You're lucky."

I nod. I *have* been lucky. To be able to be born into a life of privilege, and have the chance to still keep away from the crowds and cameras—it's something I never truly appreciated until I came here.

The children—two boys and a girl—sit on an overstuffed sofa and smile politely. The youngest, a girl, looks to be about nine years old. She's staring at Margot with wide eyes.

When we're brought to the dining room, I catch Margot winking at the little Princess. Margot takes a sweet out of her purse and hands it to the princess, putting her finger to her lips conspiratorially. The girl smiles, and my heart warms.

It's rare to see Margot acting without any guardedness.

She usually has walls up so high around her that it's hard to see the person behind them. The three kids naturally gravitate toward her, surrounding her as we make our way to the dining room.

Children and animals are the two greatest barometers when it comes to judging someone's character. Right now, watching Margot interact with the three little royals makes my heart skip a beat.

They see the same qualities in her that I do.

I know I've only met Margot a couple of weeks ago. I know the most we've done is little more than kissing. So, why is my mind racing toward a future with her?

I could see her beside me, lazing in bed on a Sunday morning with a few kids of our own one day.

Tearing my eyes away from the blonde beauty, I inhale deeply to try to keep my thoughts under control. I barely know Margot. Just because I'm drawn to her doesn't mean she's going to carry my hypothetical children.

Telling myself to get a grip is useless, though, because every time I look at her, I see a future I never thought I'd have. A future I never thought I wanted.

A future that, all of a sudden, seems possible.

14

MARGOT

WHEN WE GET BACK to our own house, Luca and Ivy disappear upstairs. I glance into the kitchen, wishing I could have a glass of wine to unwind.

It's not even just the fact that I'm pregnant. It's what happened that night with Beckett. Since he's gone on the run, I've thought that he's the one that caused my overdose, but I just don't remember. That hole in my memory tortures me, and I don't want to feel out of control again.

Part of me thinks it was Beckett's fault, somehow. The worst part is, I can't say anything about it, because no one knows that Beckett was with me. If someone found out, they might put two and two together about the baby, and, well, that would be a disaster.

Alcohol used to be my favorite vice. Now, I don't even want to touch it. Even when I'm lonely and emotional, which seems to be happening a lot these days.

Tonight, after seeing the love that the King and Queen have for each other, I feel lonelier than ever.

I head out to the pool in the backyard. With winter on the

way, the pool technician drained the pool a few inches this week. There won't be any swimming in it until next year.

I watch the vapor of my breath in the night air, letting my shoulders relax as I sink down onto a pool lounge chair. Wrapping my arms around my torso, I try to ward off the cold. In a way, it feels good to have the chill of the air seep into my bones. It makes me feel alive. Awake.

A noise behind me makes me turn my head.

"Mind if I join you?" Prince Dante asks.

I smile. "Of course not. I was just trying to unwind. Being on my best behavior tends to stress me out."

The Prince's smile widens. "I'd love to see you on your worst behavior."

"Don't know if you've earned that yet."

The Prince grins, taking a seat in the lounge chair next to mine, his hand drifting over to me. He rests it on top of mine, and the warmth of his skin sends comfort flowing through my body.

How is it possible to feel so comfortable with someone I barely know?

"Do you ever feel like we've known each other for longer than two weeks?" Dante glances at me, quirking an eyebrow.

"Like we're long-lost lovers that have somehow, against all odds, reunited at last?"

"Exactly," he grins.

I chuckle, nodding. "Yeah, actually. I do."

"At least I'm not crazy."

"I never said that," I laugh. "Maybe we're both crazy."

"Crazy isn't so bad." His fingers curl around my hand. My heart thumps.

My other hand drifts to my stomach. I want to tell Dante about the baby. I want to tell him everything. All the pain that I've been holding inside me, all the anxiety and fear, all the hopes and dreams and silly visions that I have for my future.

I want him to know everything. I want him to be a part of my future.

Is it desperate? Maybe.

It's true, though.

A lump forms in my throat, and the words stick. Closing my eyes, I let his presence comfort me until I can breathe again.

"Is it hard staying sober?"

The Prince's question surprises me. I turn my head to look at him, frowning slightly. He noticed I've been sober?

He continues: "I mean, I've seen you refuse drinks at multiple dinners. I assumed it was something with your therapy. I just thought it might be hard, considering who you are and the kind of events you have to go to."

Smiling, I shake my head. "No. It's not really that hard." With my hand still on my stomach, I think of my child. It's not hard to stay sober for my baby.

The Prince's eyebrows arch. "No?"

I chuckle. "I mean, not really. I only ever really partied, I was never a really heavy user or anything. I drank a lot at celebrity events. There are some embarrassing photos of me online."

"Yeah," Dante says, gazing at the pool.

"You've seen them?"

He stiffens, straightening up in the chair. "I mean, I don't... I'm not..."

"Have you been Googling me, Your Highness?"

Dante swings his gaze to meet mine and a grin tugs at the corner of his full, irresistible lips. "Can you blame me?"

"Find anything interesting?"

"Plenty."

His eyes linger on mine, sending pulsing heat rushing through my body. Whenever he looks at me like that, butterflies explode though my stomach. I clear my throat, tearing my gaze away from his. If I look at him much longer, I'll be climbing onto his chair and straddling him right here, right now.

I let out a sigh, shaking my head. "I have lots of reasons to stay sober. It kills me that I don't know what happened the night that I OD'd."

"Have you ever considered that it might have been Beckett?"

I gulp, keeping my gaze straight ahead. "Your Highness, I wouldn't..." If I say yes, he'll know I was with Beckett.

"Come on, Margot. My half-brother went on a murderous rampage. He was trying to get at Luca by any means possible. Why not through you?"

My mind spins circles around me. How am I supposed to answer this? If I say yes, it'll be tantamount to admitting that Beckett was with me. If I say no, I'm lying, and I've never been a good liar.

So, I settle on the truth.

"I've thought of it, but I don't know how he would have hurt me."

He nods, gazing at me. "I'll find out."

"Dante, you don't have to do that. You have enough to deal with already, between Luca and the security around here. You don't need to add me to your list of burdens."

"You're not a burden. Never."

I take a deep breath, staring up at the stars in the sky. My breath leaves little puffs of vapor, and I watch it dissipate. The Prince squeezes my hand.

"I mean it, Margot. I care about you."

"Long-lost lovers," I whisper, staring up at the night sky.

The truth is on the tip of my tongue. The Prince has shoved a wedge in the cage around my heart, and he's slowly prying it open. I could open my mouth and tell him everything.

My diagnosis. The night I found out. The baby. Beckett. My suspicions about my overdose.

I can't get the words out, though. I'm scared of losing what little affection he has for me.

"Hey," Dante whispers, tugging at my arm. I turn to look at him, feeling the wedge in my chest split the cage open another fraction of an inch. His eyes are so kind. They make me want to spill my secrets, to share my entire life with him.

It wouldn't be that hard. In a few words, I could rid myself of this awful burden. I could tell him everything. It's like he said—it feels like we've known each other forever. Maybe he wouldn't turn me away. Maybe I wouldn't lose him. Maybe it would bring us closer together.

He opens his mouth to speak, but the back door of the house slides open.

Felicity, my publicist, calls out my name. She comes running across the grass toward us.

"Margot! I've been trying to call you!"

"I don't have my phone."

Throwing an apologetic glance at the Prince, I get up off the lounge chair. Felicity huffs, leaning on the pool fence. When she sees the Prince, her eyes widen. She curtsies awkwardly and then turns to me. "Hunter gave an interview."

My ribs squeeze. The Prince slides his hand over my lower back, and I lean into him for comfort.

Felicity glances at him, and then back at me. "He told the *Enquirer* that you're pregnant. I've drafted a statement to deny it, but..." She chews her lip, glancing at my stomach.

"But you want to know if it's true or not," I finish for her.

Felicity nods, and the Prince freezes beside me.

"He published medical records," Felicity says, frowning. "They could be fake, but..."

My heart sinks. I wish I could have had a few more weeks with him. Maybe even just a few more days, the way things are going. I wish I could have laid in bed beside him and felt his naked body next to mine. I would have loved to have felt him inside me just once—just to feel what it's like to orgasm with a man like him.

But now, I'll never know.

The news will never bring us closer together. Once he finds out I'm pregnant, he'll never want to keep up this... whatever this is between us.

I take a deep breath, dragging my eyes up to Felicity's. I nod.

Her face falls. "Margot..."

"Just over eighteen weeks," I say, running my hand over my stomach.

The Prince hasn't said a word. His hand is still on my back, but I can sense the uneasiness pulsing from him. Gathering all my courage, I force myself to look at him.

I gulp. "I'm sorry I didn't tell you."

Tears sting my eyes.

The Prince shakes his head, sliding his hand around to hold my waist. "You were never obligated to tell me."

Felicity clears her throat. "Is His Highness the father?" Her eyes dart from me to Dante and back to me again.

I shake my head. "No."

"Who...?"

"It's not important. He's not in the picture."

Felicity lets out a breath. "Well, this complicates things."

I snort. "I know it does. But that's why you get paid the big bucks, Felicity."

"What am I going to tell your sponsors?"

"Tell them I'm going to be a mother," I shrug.

"So...you're keeping it?"

I stare at my publicist, letting her words sink in. Heat rises to my head and I feel like steam is blowing out of my ears. "Of course I'm keeping it, Felicity. This baby saved my life. This baby is the one good thing about my life right now." I gulp, stealing a glance at the Prince. "Well, one of very few good things. It's everything to me. To be honest with you, I don't care about the sponsorships, or this house, or what you'll say to news outlets or what you want to post to my social media. Do whatever you want. Excuse me."

I nod to the Prince, slipping past Felicity and making my way into the house. My heart is racing and my face feels hot. I clench my fists, climbing the steps up to the second floor as blood pounds in my ears.

I can hear Ivy and Luca kissing in the living room, and it only makes me feel worse.

I'm alone.

Again.

I was a fool to think it could work out. I was an idiot to let Dante get close to me.

It'll never work out. His murderous half-brother is the father of my child, and the minute he learns about it, he won't want anything to do with me.

It's not until I'm undressed and under a hot shower that I let my shoulders relax. I cradle my tiny baby bump, sending all my love and strength inward.

Then, I realize that I'm not alone. I'll never be alone.

I have my baby.

15

DANTE

I WATCH Margot walk away in stunned silence. Her publicist stares as well, and then turns her gaze to me.

"Did you know?"

I shake my head. "No."

Scanning my body, I try to figure out what I'm feeling. Shocked, of course. Protective.

A little turned on?

The thought of Margot being a mother makes my heart thump. I saw the pain in her eyes when she looked at me—but also the determination.

Now, I feel like I understand the strength inside her. I understand how she can face her fears, her anxieties, and her worries. I understand how she can recover from her past and keep moving forward.

She's a mother.

To my surprise, that fact doesn't change my opinion of her, or how attracted I am to her. I watch Margot walk into the house as my heart grows in my chest.

I nod to the publicist and follow Margot inside. Voices

draw me toward the living room, and I see Luca and Ivy in deep discussion. They both look up when I walk in.

Ivy's face is tight. She gives me a small smile. "You found out about Margot?"

"Did you know?"

They both nod. I frown at Luca. "You didn't tell me?"

He shrugs. "It wasn't my news to tell."

I sit with them, leaning against the sofa as I mull over this development. How does this impact Beckett and his attack on Luca? Is Margot in more danger now, or less?

Luca answers my unsaid question. "We'll keep security tight on the two girls," he says, nodding to me. "And continue trying to draw Beckett out to face us. Now, more than ever, it's important that we keep Ivy and Margot safe. Who knows—maybe the news will be enough to get Beckett to show himself. Maybe he'll think it's mine."

Tension ratchets up in my body at the thought of Luca touching Margot.

I take a deep breath. "Theo said they're not having much luck searching Argyle. He's had to open the ports and let planes fly on a normal schedule again, but security is still tight."

"Who knows where Beckett is?" Luca shakes his head.

"I'm more worried about Hunter." Ivy wrings her hands, staring between us. "Did you read the article? He was clearly vindictive and hoping that revealing Margot's pregnancy would cause her pain. He even said she wasn't fit to be a mother and took a jab at her sponsorships and brand partners, saying they should drop her."

"Is he the father?" I try to ask the question casually, even though my throat tightens. The thought of a vindictive, hateful man like Hunter being the father of Margot's child makes me sick. If he would willingly poison Ivy's bakery just to spite her, who knows what he would do to his own child.

Ivy barks out a laugh, shaking her head. "I seriously doubt it. Margot wouldn't touch him with a ten-foot pole."

"So, you don't know who the father is?"

Ivy shakes her head. "Haven't been able to get it out of her."

"Maybe she doesn't know." Luca runs his fingers through his hair.

"Let's stop gossiping." Ivy sighs, shaking her head. "We need to figure out what we're going to do about this, and if it affects this whole mess with Beckett in any way."

"Well, it might make Margot a target. He could see her as a weak point," I say, lacing my fingers behind my head.

"She won't want to leave the house." Ivy chews her lip, sliding her hand into Luca's. "And this is happening just when she was starting to be herself again. Margot's been so sad for so long, and just these past couple of weeks, I've seen the old Margot come out. She's been happier. Calmer. She's actually *smiled* multiple times."

Ivy lets out a heavy sigh. My knee bounces up and down, and I glance toward the staircase. It feels wrong to be talking about Margot without her here. We should be comforting her, not outlining our security plans without her.

I excuse myself and stand up. Heading up the stairs, I turn toward Margot's end of the hallway instead of my own. As I stand at her door, I raise my fist to knock.

I hesitate.

Who am I to offer her comfort? I'm just a guy who's been living with her for a few weeks. Sure, we've kissed—and done a little bit more—but does she actually want to see me?

With a deep breath, I ignore my hesitation and rap my knuckles on the door.

"Yeah?" Margot's voice calls out on the other side.

"It's me." I lean my forehead against the door, praying that she'll let me in.

When I hear her footsteps on the other side, my breath catches. I lift my head as she opens the door, my heart racing behind my ribs. I stare into her bright, blue eyes, wanting nothing more than to wrap my arms around her and tell her it'll be okay.

It's not like me to be this sentimental. It's not like me to search out someone just to comfort them. I've spent my entire life on my own, and it's never bothered me.

But Margot is different. She's gotten under my skin, and I need to make sure she's okay. Her pain feels like my pain, and until I know that she's feeling all right, I won't be able to do anything.

"Hey," she says, opening the door wider.

I step inside, inhaling the scent of her that clings to every surface of her bedroom. She gestures to a plush chair for me to sit and takes a seat at her vanity.

She's wearing a light blue silk pajama set. The sight of the matching camisole and shorts makes my mouth water, even though I know it's not the time to be thinking about these things.

What can I say? The woman's put a spell on me.

The thin, silky camisole looks like it would feel like heaven to touch—and even better to take off.

I watch as she picks up a jar of something, taking a small amount and patting it around her eyes. Her back is straight as a rod, and her chin is high as she stares at herself in the mirror.

"Are you okay?" I ask, not knowing how else to break the silence.

Margot taps the skin around her eyes with her ring finger,

not meeting my gaze. "I'm fine. It's better that everyone knows." She finally drags her eyes over to mine. "I'm sorry I didn't tell you."

"You don't owe me anything."

"I wanted you to know about the baby. I would have liked to tell you some other way." The depth of the pain in her eyes makes me pause.

I gulp past a lump of jagged rocks that has taken up residence at the base of my throat. Shaking my head, I reach across the vanity to put my hand on her forearm.

"I don't care how I found out."

"Why are you here?" she asks, holding my gaze. Her eyes are hard. Guarded. Suspicious.

"What do you mean?"

"I'm pregnant with another man's baby, and you've come up to my room to ask me if I'm okay. Why?"

I frown. I can see the walls building up around Margot's heart, brick by brick, second by second.

"Because I care about you, Margot." My voice is soft. I can feel her pulse thumping in her arm, sending waves of heat through my hand.

Margot's eyes drop back down. She takes a finger and traces the edge of my hand, chewing her lip. "How can you care about me if you've only known me a couple of weeks?"

"I don't know. I just do."

"Maybe you have a savior complex," she says, almost speaking to herself. "You're just looking for someone to save, and who better than a pregnant woman with no partner?"

"Maybe I have a Margot complex, and everything you do makes me want to spend more time with you."

My blonde goddess finally drags her eyes up to mine. They're filled with tears. I stand up, pulling her up with me and squeezing her into my chest.

"I'm a mess, Dante," she says into my shirt. "I'm pregnant and alone. I have anxiety, and..." She sighs, stopping herself. "My career is about to fall apart, and I'm going to lose all this. I'm trapped in this life, Your Highness. I'm locked inside it, and I'm looking at a long, long fall down to the bottom. You shouldn't be spending more time with me. You should be running away."

"I'm not running away from anything. I'm not afraid of falling."

How can I explain to her that she's everything I never knew I needed? How can I tell her that I've never met anyone who is so brave, so strong, and so perfect in all her flaws? She makes me realize everything I've been missing by hiding myself away from the public. She makes me feel like there's so much more life to live, if only I could gather the courage to reach out and grab it.

How can I tell her that after only a couple of weeks, I feel like I'm already falling for her?

Words aren't enough. Even if I knew the right ones to say, I wouldn't be able to speak them with the tightening in my throat. Instead, I take my finger and gently tilt Margot's chin up toward me.

When I press my lips against hers, she lets out a soft whimper. Her body is tense, and for a painful moment, I think she's going to pull away. I'm going to lose her before I even had her to begin with.

Instead, though, Margot's lips part and she melts into me. The walls she's been building come crumbling down, and my heart beats with hers.

16

MARGOT

When Dante kisses me, nothing else seems to matter. Not the baby growing inside me, not the death of career, not the fact that his half-brother is the father of my child.

Not my illness, or the fact that I'm looking down the barrel of a long, painful future.

The only thing that matters are his hands on my waist, his lips on mine, and the growing need in the pit of my stomach.

Thoughts disappear from my mind. Tension evaporates in my body, and the only thing that exists is the pleasure that Dante promises.

Pleasure that I haven't experienced in a long time.

Pleasure that I've even denied giving myself.

Taking my hand, the Prince leads me over to the big four-poster bed. He lays me on top of the goose down blanket, his eyes running down the length of my body.

Everywhere he looks, little bursts of electricity erupt over my skin. Goosebumps sweep over me from head to toe. The Prince slides his hand over the silky fabric of my pajamas, groaning as he feels my pebbled nipple.

Pulling the neckline down to reveal my breast, he drops

his mouth to taste it. As soon as his warm tongue swipes over my nipple, a gasp escapes my lips.

Fire rushes down my spine, swirling around my stomach and teasing between my thighs. It only takes one touch for Dante to make me feel alive again.

Maybe I've denied myself pleasure because I knew he would come into my life. Maybe, deep down, I knew there would be a Prince to come save me from this life I've been imprisoned in. All these years that I've avoided pleasure happened to make this moment all the sweeter.

All this time, I've been waiting for him. My Dante.

Laying kisses down over my breasts, my chest, my collarbone, the Prince moves back up to kiss my lips. He claims them, his small bit of stubble scratching my skin as he peppers me with kisses. Every sense is heightened. Every nerve ending is screaming for his touch, his lips, his everything.

I run my fingers over his shoulders and down his sides, pulling his shirt off over his head. Trailing my hands over his body, I exhale as I feel the warm, hard muscles his clothes have been hiding.

Even the sight of his chest makes my pulse hammer. I gulp, my mouth watering at the bulge in his pants.

When I reach for his belt buckle, Dante chuckles. He pushes my hand away, dragging my own camisole off over my head. Pinning my arms above my head, he crushes his lips to mine. He lays claim to my mouth, and I love every second of it.

Spreading my knees, I roll my hips to feel the hardness of his shaft.

An ache grows between my legs. An emptiness that only he can fill.

With both my wrists held in one of his hands over my

head, the Prince sweeps his other hand down my body. I gasp when he tugs my nipple, sending another wave of shivers tumbling down my body. Heat sparks between my thighs as my need grows more intense.

When the Prince slips his hand under my silk pajama shorts, I sink my teeth into his shoulder. He groans when he feels my wetness, not hesitating to slip his fingers inside me.

Gasping, I arch my back.

Pinning me to the bed, the Prince teases me with his fingers. I say he teases me, because I already know that fingers won't be enough for me tonight.

Even when heat builds in the pit of my stomach, and he moves to pleasure my clit. Even when his fingers dance like magic between my legs, and when his hot breath washes over my skin. Even when he bites my earlobe, driving his fingers deep inside me and touching a spot inside me I didn't even know existed.

When my body trembles and an orgasm crashes into me, leaving me limp and broken on the bed, I still know it won't be enough.

Dante slips his fingers out of me and drags them across my lips.

"Taste yourself," he commands in a hoarse whisper.

I suck his fingers inside my mouth, tasting my own orgasm on them. I swirl my tongue around as the need inside me crests.

As soon as he releases my wrists from his grasp, I flip Dante onto his back. I'm shaking as I unhook his belt and shimmy his pants down his legs.

Tearing my own shorts off, I straddle the Prince. His hard, gorgeous shaft pulses against me.

I suck my bottom lip into my mouth, looking up at Dante's face. Hooded, dark eyes stare back at me. With my hands braced on his chest, I can feel his heart hammering behind his ribcage. I rock my hips, gasping as his cock nestles in my slit.

I'm torn between desperately wanting him inside me, and needing this moment to last. Right now, the only thing that matters is pleasure. I have no anxieties and no circling thoughts. I have no crushing weight on my chest, and no dread seeping into my soul.

I just have pleasure, cradled in the pit of my stomach, ready to be unleashed.

Reaching down between us, I angle the Prince toward my opening. His lips drop open, his hands moving to my thighs.

"Margot," he whispers.

"Yeah?"

I don't wait for an answer. I can't wait. Dropping my hips, I spear myself with him. We both moan in unison, his fingers sinking into my flesh as I curl my hands into his shoulders.

My body screams for him. Our bodies slam together as the energy becomes frantic. Wild. Animalistic.

The Prince doesn't say anything. He grunts, pulling my hips closer as he drives himself inside me. I ride him, laughter bubbling up inside me as pleasure mounts in my veins.

It's never felt like this before.

Never so intense. So needy. So fucking good.

Everywhere his hands touch, sparks fly. The Prince moves his hands from my thighs to my ass, spreading my cheeks wide as he drives himself deeper inside me.

I moan, gripping the headboard as our movements become frenzied. The Prince slaps my ass before rocking himself inside me harder.

I let go.

I let go of everything that's ever held me back, everything

that's stopped me from feeling pleasure, everything that has kept me locked away in my own towering fear.

My orgasm crashes into me like a high-speed train. It annihilates me, splitting me in half as the Prince drives himself inside me.

I think I scream. I don't know.

All I know is that my fingers leave deep, red scratch marks on the Prince's chest. His cock fits perfectly inside me, like it was made to be there. Heat explodes inside me, making my body arch and convulse as another scream rips through my throat.

When I feel the Prince's cock get harder, another wave of pleasure crashes into me. He splashes his seed inside me, and I give myself to him completely.

Mind, body, and soul.

When it's over, I collapse on the bed beside him. My hair splays out around me and I rest my arm against my forehead. My chest heaves, and my entire body trembles and twitches.

Prince Dante lays a palm on my thigh as he tries to catch his breath.

Little tingles flow through my veins, making my body twitch with the after-effects of my orgasm. I roll onto my side, trailing my fingers over Dante's chest.

Sighing, I shake my head. "That was nice."

"I'm just getting started," the Prince grins. He pulls me closer, laying my head on his chest. Closing my eyes, I listen to his heartbeat and let calm and happiness overtake my spirit.

As I lay there, listening, there's only one thought on my mind:

I wish Dante was the father.

17

DANTE

WAKING up next to Margot is a pleasure I never knew I was missing. Her head is resting on my chest, with her fingers twitching gently as she dreams. I lay a kiss on her golden hair, sighing.

Before coming to Farcliff, I was content in my quiet, isolated existence. I thought I was happy.

I had no idea what was missing from my life. I never imagined that I could want to spend time with someone else as much as I want to with Margot.

She stirs in my arms, sighing softly. Smiling at me, Margot stretches out and rolls onto her pillows.

"I had such a good sleep."

"Same."

"Haven't slept that well in years."

"Must be the orgasms," I grin.

Margot laughs. "Must be. Wouldn't mind another one," she grins.

"That can be arranged."

"You've created a monster," she laughs, wrapping her arms around me. "Look what you've unleashed."

I growl, and Margot lets out another giggle.

I never knew I could love hearing someone laugh as much as I love hearing it from Margot.

"Hold on," she says when I move to kiss her. "Morning breath."

I watch her pad to the ensuite bathroom to brush her teeth. When I hear the shower turn on, I get out of bed and join her.

We fit so well together. Both of us appreciate comfortable silence. We don't have to talk. I hate going out to drink and party, and Margot doesn't do any of those things. We've slipped into each other's lives so effortlessly, it's easy to forget the things that loom just ahead.

Her baby, for one. Am I really ready to have a child in my life? Is it crazy that I'm really considering it?

Seeing Ivy and Luca be so joyous about their own twins makes me itch to have that for myself.

Besides the baby, though, there's Beckett to worry about. We still have no news on his whereabouts, and he could pop up at any time and try to hurt Luca.

Then, there's Hunter. Margot's agent has a bone to pick with her, and judging by the interview he gave last night, it sounds like he's out for blood.

I'm willingly inserting myself into all those problems.

For what, though? Why would I do that?

As soon as I push the bathroom door open and see Margot smiling at me from the shower, I have my answer. I'm doing it for her.

Joining her under the stream of water, I wrap my arms around her, pulling her into me so her back rests against my chest. Running my hands over her stomach, my heart thumps at the thought of the life that's growing inside.

As Margot puts her hands on top of mine, it feels like everything in my life clicks into place.

I want her. I want the baby. I want to take all the publicity and the cameras and the invasions of privacy if it means I get to hold Margot in my arms at the end of the day.

It hardly makes sense to me—she represents everything that I've avoided since I was a kid.

But the heart wants what the heart wants, and I want Margot LeBlanc.

Spinning in my arms, Margot slides her hands up to tangle into my hair. She pulls me down and kisses me tenderly. Steam billows around us and the shower pours down onto us.

Our hearts beat against each other, and I feel whole.

I'M WALKING on air for the next week. Margot and I don't go out much. Her publicist puts out a statement acknowledging her pregnancy, but we stay out of view of the cameras. We don't watch television, and our phones stay locked away in a drawer.

It's mid-November, and the holiday spirit is starting to take hold. There's music and decorations and a buzz in the air. Or maybe that's just how I feel?

In a way, my life in Farcliff feels just like my life did in Argyle. I spend time with Luca, Ivy, and most importantly, Margot. I keep in contact with Theo through email, and make sure the security teams are working as they're supposed to.

Besides that, I make love to Margot often and wholeheartedly. As the days go on, we become more comfortable with each other. It just feels *right*.

A week after Hunter's revelation in the media, Margot and I decide to go to the bakery to visit Ivy and Luca. We drive ourselves there, bringing only two bodyguards. The streets are quiet, and Luca tells me most of the media attention around Margot has died down.

Just like anything, her pregnancy is a juicy bit of gossip that will pass. The media will latch onto something else. Everything will work out.

We make it to Ivy's bakery, slipping in the back door. Ivy puts us to work immediately and Margot smiles, throwing me a sideways glance.

"If there was anyone who can make you forget that you're a celebrity or royalty, it's my sister."

"I never felt like royalty anyway, so I don't mind," I grin.

Margot's cheeks are glowing, and the way she smiles at me makes my heart grow in my chest. I help her bring a few big boxes out to the dumpsters out back, and then wrap my arms around her waist. We're alone out here, behind the building.

Stealing a kiss, I run my hands over Margot's ass.

"I can't wait to see your body change," I growl. "Is it wrong that it turns me on that you're pregnant?"

"I wouldn't say it's wrong," Margot laughs, nuzzling her nose to mine. "Fortunate for me, though."

"The thought of your belly growing, your tits getting swollen and heavy..." I growl, nipping at her bottom lip.

She laughs, pulling away to look me in the eye. "You don't care that it's not yours?"

Margot bites her lip, staring into my eyes. I can tell that even though the question just slipped out of her, it's something she's been thinking about for a while.

I take a deep breath, not wanting to say the wrong thing. "No," I finally say. "I don't."

"That's a big responsibility to be taking on when you've known me, what? A month?"

"I know." I inhale deeply, pulling her closer. "I can't explain it, Margot, I just feel like we're meant to be together. Did you know that I wasn't even going to come to Farcliff? Theo was going to send his personal security advisor, but at the last minute I got over my fear of leaving and decided to come myself. It's like something compelled me to come to Farcliff. Theo was shocked that I would even consider it, let alone want to come up here."

"Your brother's safety compelled you," Margot smiles. "Not some destiny to meet me." She shakes her head, running her fingers through my hair. "I just don't want you to get into something and regret it later. I...I don't want to get my hopes up. I'd resigned myself to doing this alone, and now..."

"Now, you have hope," I finish for her.

Margot nods. "Hope is scary."

"I'm here."

"Just take a few days to think about it, Dante. Please." Margot's eyebrows draw together. "Really think about what it means to be with me and my baby. If it's too much, I'd rather know now."

I want to tell her that I've already thought about it. I already know what my answer will be. But the look in her eye stops me. I gulp, nodding.

"Okay. I'll think about it."

Margot's shoulders relax, and she lays a soft kiss on my lips. "Thank you."

I smile, taking her hand and leading her inside. If only she knew that every kiss she gives me, every look she throws my way, every touch of her skin against mine—it just makes me more sure that she's the one I want to be with.

I'm dizzy with emotion when we walk back into the bakery's front room. Luca, Ivy, and her friends the twins all glance at us.

Ivy sucks her bottom lip between her teeth, slowly turning her phone toward Margot.

Margot's eyes widen, and she turns the screen to me.

It's a picture of her and me by the dumpsters, kissing. It must have been taken and posted only a few minutes ago, and it's already blowing up.

Is Prince Dante the Father?

My heart starts thumping as my thoughts get cloudy. Nausea starts rising inside me and I grip the edge of the counter to steady myself.

The comments under the picture are vicious.

She's such a slut. All she wants is a prince like her sister.

Why would he want to be with a recovering drug addict? Didn't she go to rehab after an overdose? Her baby is probably sick, anyway.

Isn't Prince Dante a recluse? I heard that he killed someone when he was a kid, and that's why he refuses to make public appearances.

Prince Dante is so ugly I want to barf.

The LeBlanc sisters are such gold diggers. I feel bad for the Argyle Princes.

I know I shouldn't care. Why would it matter what some random person on the internet thinks of me?

Somehow, though, it *does* matter. Strangers' words cut me deep, just like they did all those years ago. I hate seeing hateful comments. I hate seeing them criticize Margot, when she's the strongest and best person I've ever met. I hate seeing spiteful words from people I've never met.

It makes me feel sick.

I'm still not used to my face in the media. I've spent so

long keeping my privacy sacred, staying hidden away, that I don't know how to react.

Then, the front door of the bakery bursts open, and a dozen cameras start flashing. They come rushing at us, screaming and howling as they take picture after picture of us. Margot shields her face, turning to the back of the bakery and slipping through the door.

I stand there, stunned.

Cameras flash in my face. Paparazzi reach over the counter, grabbing at me and screaming questions.

It's not until Luca grabs me and drags me to the back that my body starts functioning again. I stumble over my feet, catching myself on the edge of the door before slipping to the relative serenity of the kitchens.

Margot has her hands over her face.

Luca stares at me.

I just stand there.

Margot's words sink in, then, and I understand what she meant when she asked me if this was what I really wanted. She wasn't only talking about her and the baby. She was talking about everything else, too.

Am I ready to give up my privacy? To be with the biggest star in Farcliff? Am I ready to be photographed and talked about, to be torn apart by the media and stared at under a microscope every time I go outside?

For the first time since I met Margot, I'm not sure.

I don't know if I can handle a stampede of photographers bursting through the door every day. I'm not sure I can handle questions about the baby's father, questions about my decisions, questions about my feelings for Margot.

Sure, my phone has lived in a drawer and I've avoided reading anything online since Hunter's story broke, but that doesn't solve anything.

Do I really want this to be my life from now on? Hiding in back rooms because I'm afraid of being trampled by bloodthirsty photographers?

When Margot drops her hands from her face and meets my gaze, I know she can read me like a book.

She already knows I'm not sure, and I watch her heart break in front of me.

18

MARGOT

I SHOULD HAVE KNOWN it was too good to be true.

The minute Prince Dante walked into my life, I should have been the one running in the other direction. My therapist has been telling me to live my life with as much routine as possible. Avoid extreme emotions. Keep myself out of situations that might cause me to harm myself until I'm strong enough to handle them.

And what do I do?

I run head-first into Prince Dante's arms.

Cracks splinter across my heart as Dante stares at me across the bakery. The distance between us grows, and I'm not sure anything can bridge it.

How stupid of me to think that he would want my child! He doesn't even know me!

How could I presume that another man would step into that role? Why would he?

Not only that, how could I ask Prince Dante to give up the life he's created for himself for me? Being with me is so much more complicated than being with anyone else. I'm damaged, in more ways than one, and all my flaws are displayed for the whole world to see.

He doesn't even know the biggest flaw of all. He doesn't know the secret that I've been hiding from everyone, including Ivy.

I turn away from him. I can't withstand his stare any longer. His eyes are like an assault on my heart, throwing dagger after dagger into my chest.

Taking a trembling breath, I try to talk myself down. At least this happened now, and not after the baby is born. At least I have a few months to get used to being on my own again. At least I know how he feels for sure.

Isn't it better to know now, than to find out later?

Then why does it hurt so fucking bad?

I lean against one of the stainless steel trolleys, sucking a breath in through my teeth. I slide a hand over my stomach, drawing strength from the life growing inside me.

I always knew I was on my own. All Prince Dante gave me was a quick distraction.

That's what I tell myself, anyway. I ignore the pain in my chest as my heart starts to break all over again.

Alone, alone, alone.

He doesn't even know the truth about my disease. Once he finds out, he'll run. I know he will. And it'll be my fault, because I didn't have the guts to tell him.

Guilty, guilty, guilty.

Then, a warm, strong hand sweeps over my back. I inhale Prince Dante's scent, leaning into his touch. He spins me around to face him, cupping my cheek in his hand.

When he crushes his lips against mine, I sob. The Prince wipes my tears away with his thumbs, kissing me harder. Trembling against him, I don't want to give in to the love he's offering.

I want to lock myself away and never see anyone again. I want to suffer on my own. I never want to feel this disappointment again. Even for the few moments when I thought he was walking away, it hurt too much to face.

But Prince Dante wraps his arms around me, and I have no choice—I never had a choice with him. As soon as he walked into my life, he had my heart in the palm of his hand.

Pulling away from his kiss, I stare into the Prince's eyes.

"What are you doing?"

"Kissing you."

"Why?"

"Because you deserve to be kissed." His body is hard as he pulls me closer. His arms circle protectively around me, and I feel safer than I've ever felt before.

He wants to be let in, but I'm still hiding so much. Beckett is the father, and I have an incurable disease. I don't deserve his love.

Guilty, guilty, guilty.

Another tear falls from my eye, and he kisses it away. "Stop crying."

"I thought you didn't want this. The media. The gossip." My breath hitches, and I force myself to say what I want to say. "The baby."

Instead of answering, Prince Dante tucks a strand of hair behind my ear. "Come away with me."

"What?"

"Come back to Argyle. Get away from Farcliff and all this paparazzi. Let me show you where I come from."

My heart stutters.

The Prince's eyes soften. "I care about you, Margot. I know it hasn't been long, but I feel like meeting you was meant to be."

He slips his hands into mine, staring into my eyes.

I take a deep breath, forcing a smile. "My whole life, I've been used by other people. Whether they meant to do it or not, it's what's happened. I was pulled out of school to start modeling. My father used me to generate income for himself. Then, everyone that I thought was a friend was just climbing over me to get more fame and fortune."

The Prince tilts his head, listening. His hold on my waist tightens, and I feel a wave of affection rolling off him.

"The only person that I thought I could trust was Ivy, which is why it hurt me so badly when I felt like she had just used me to start her own bakery. Even my agent, Hunter, had worked with me for years. I knew being his client was a business relationship, but we worked together for so many years that I thought he genuinely cared about me. I was wrong." I smile sadly. "That's why it's hard for me to believe you when you say you care about me."

"What can I do to prove it to you?"

"You don't have to prove it to me, Dante." I shake my head, running my hands up his chest. "I just need to work through it in my own mind."

"Does that mean you won't come to Argyle?"

"I will," I say slowly. "But I just need a few days to breathe. I don't want to run away from the media. I don't want to run away from my problems. My therapist says that I should sit with uncomfortable feelings instead of trying to mask them."

Working on yourself is difficult. Facing your worst qualities and trying to improve them takes real effort, and not many people are willing to do it. I have to do it—for my sake and my child's. I just hope Dante understands.

As soon as a smile tugs at his lips, I know he gets it. He nods, laying a gentle kiss on my lips. "You're so strong, Margot. It never ceases to amaze me."

I laugh, shaking my head. "I don't feel strong."

A security guard comes in the back door of the bakery, striding toward the two of us. "Your car is ready," he says with a nod.

Luca dips his chin down at Dante and me. "Ivy and I will be back tonight. I'm going to stay here with her. I don't like leaving her with this many people in the bakery."

"See you tonight," Dante says to his brother. He takes my hand and leads me through the back door. There are a slew of reporters waiting for us, but instead of hiding away from them, Dante flashes a smile. He waves to the cameras, and my heart grows.

This is the first time I've seen him comfortable in the public eye. Holding my hand and leading me to the car, he carries himself like a true Prince. The defenses I've built around my heart start to weaken, because I know the Prince is doing this for me. If it were up to him, he'd be hiding away in a palace in Argyle. The only reason he's smiling for the cameras is because he wants to make me feel comfortable.

I don't remember the last time someone did something like that for me.

Sure, I've been to lavish parties, and I've been paid for my time and presence. I've received boxes and boxes of gifts from companies. I've had people tell me what they think I've wanted to hear. I've been given the world.

I've never had someone stand beside me as proudly as Dante stands now, doing something that he hates, just because he wants to show me that he cares.

As we slide into the car, the Prince lets out a heavy sigh. He throws me a glance, shaking his head. "I don't know how you do it. I was only in front of the cameras for a few seconds, and I feel exhausted."

I smile, leaning my head on his shoulder.

I told him that he didn't need to prove to me that he cared

about me, but in those ten seconds from the door of the bakery to the car, he showed me more than he realizes. He put himself in an uncomfortable situation and stood by my side, even when he didn't have to.

My heart thuds in my chest. I believe Dante when he says he cares about me. It makes me feel exhilarated and alive...

...and vulnerable.

Thinking that he cares about me opens me up to so much heartache.

But I listen to my therapist's words. I sit with the uncomfortable feeling, knowing that I can get through it. Knowing it won't last. Knowing that whatever lies on the other side is worth it.

19

DANTE

Media circus DOESN'T COME CLOSE to describing the two weeks that follow the picture of Margot and me. For the thousandth time, I realize how lucky I've been in Argyle.

Sitting in the living room with Luca, I watch through the windows as a member of our security team tackles a photographer to the ground in the backyard. His camera goes skidding across the patio, and another photographer's head pops up above the hedge.

Click, click, click.

Even from inside, I can hear the camera's shutter—but that might just be an echo in my mind. For the past two weeks, I've been dreaming of the sounds of cameras, and waking up thinking a flash is going off in my bedroom.

"I think we might need to move," Luca grins, glancing at me. "I thought you being here was supposed to help my security situation."

"So did I."

The security guard lifts the photographer off the ground, throwing him over his shoulder as another guard rushes to the hedges. Within seconds, the privacy in the backyard is restored. With every day that goes by, the paparazzi are getting more and more daring.

My face, which was once hidden from the public, is now on every newspaper. My name, once a footnote in the history of Argyle, is plastered all over the headlines.

Being a recluse has had the opposite effect that I wanted. Now that my name is front and center, people only want to know more.

I glance at my brother. "At least if it's me in the news, it takes the heat off you."

Luca chuckles, shaking his head. He sighs, staring out at the now-empty backyard. "We can't live like this. Let me call in a favor."

My brother pulls out his phone. When he says the name 'Damon,' I frown. Does he mean Prince Damon? I listen to him say a few words on the phone before hanging up. He glances at me, nodding.

"The royal family of Farcliff will prepare a wing for the four of us at the castle. We'll be safer up there."

I let out a sigh. Moving to the castle means relinquishing a lot of control over the security team we have here. If Beckett was able to attempt to murder Luca in the castle once before, what's to say that he can't do it again?

But as a big, burly security guard talks into his earpiece outside, scanning the tops of the hedges surrounding Margot's property, I know it has to be done.

It's no longer safe for us to stay here.

Luca stretches out on the sofa, staring at me. "So, you and Margot, hey?"

I shrug. "Yeah."

"You know, I kind of thought you were into men when we

were growing up. You never had a girlfriend, never talked about girls, nothing."

I chuckle. "Did you?"

"Yeah, Theo and I talked about it before my accident. We thought you might have been scared to come out to us."

I shake my head. "Nah. Just never met someone I liked. I preferred to be alone most of the time. Or at least, that's what I told myself."

Luca grunts. "You took the whole thing with Mother really badly."

My face sours. I've told Margot a bit about what happened with our mother, but not the whole story. When our mother cheated on our father, it caused a splash in the papers. When it came out that our father's brother was her lover, the media were relentless.

When Beckett was born, photographers stormed the castle and every event where our family would be attending. They were vicious and completely shameless.

One morning, I woke up with a photographer climbing through my bedroom window. I had nightmares for weeks, and it started off the whole chain of events that led to my barfing all over my ceremonial uniform and becoming Argyle's first meme.

Then, our mother, the Queen, ran off with our uncle, leaving all four of us kids to fend for ourselves with an angry father and a ruthless pack of reporters.

I shake my head. "I never understood how you could forgive Mother. And then Cara..." I trail off, not wanting to open old wounds for my brother.

To my surprise, Luca smiles. "You can choose to be guarded and lonely, or you can take life as it comes. I spent a few years angry and bitter about Cara's betrayal, but when I think about it now, it's what brought Ivy into my life. It's what will make me a father. I could never be bitter about that."

MOVING to Farcliff Castle happens quickly. Prince Damon sends a car for us that same evening, and Luca, Ivy, Margot, and I move to the luxury of the royal estate. As soon as we cross the gates into the royal grounds, the air changes.

I no longer feel the ever-present eye of the reporters, but instead, the pressure of court life. Farcliff is much more formal than Argyle, and I immediately want Margot to take up my offer to show her what my home Kingdom is like.

With winter now in full swing in Farcliff, I'm craving some warm weather and palm trees.

The four of us are led to our own guest wing of the castle. Luca is given the same room he was in before, and I'm housed next door. The two girls are across the hall from us.

I glance around the room at the affluence, sighing. A massive four-poster bed dominates the room, with big double doors leading to an ensuite bathroom. The taps in the bathroom are gold, with little gold accents all around the room. Everything is ornate, opulent, over-the top.

A quiet knock sounds on the door. I open it to see Margot staring back at me with a soft smile on her face.

"Hi," she says.

"Hi, gorgeous."

"Thank you for organizing this. It's nice to not have to worry about cameras being shoved in my face."

"It was all Luca," I say, opening the door wider for her to come in.

I wrap my arms around Margot, once again feeling the warmth seep into my heart. She leans her head against my chest, sighing.

"You smell good," she says, her voice muffled against my shirt.

"So do you," I grin.

We fall into bed together, and for the first time in a couple of weeks, I'm not worried about her safety. I let go of the fears of being watched, and the anxiety that has crept into my heart over the past month.

I just make love to a beautiful woman, and let my feelings for her grow.

We lay tangled in each other's arms, and I feel happy.

THE NEXT DAY, I slip my hand into Margot's and bring her outside. As we walk through the well-manicured gardens, I let my shoulders relax. It's been many weeks since we were able to walk together without looking over our shoulder. Even the thought of someone attacking Luca fades from my mind, and I let myself be quiet, happy, and calm.

We walk into the lush forest that surrounds the castle, eventually walking to the edge of Farcliff Lake. We stand on the shore, silent. She leans her head against my shoulder and I wrap my arm around her waist.

I've never felt so comfortable with someone else, ever. I always felt like being around other people was an effort. It was draining. I had to try hard, and then once I was alone, I had to recharge my energy until I was ready to speak to people again.

I thought people were exhausting. I thought I was destined to spend my life mostly in isolation.

Not with Margot.

When she's with me, it feels better than being alone.

She glances at me, her eyes shining. "I'd like to go to Argyle," she finally says.

"Yeah? What made you change your mind?"

"Ivy doesn't need me here. She has Luca. I think, maybe, moving out of my comfort zone would be a good thing." She glances back the way we came, toward the castle. "Plus, being at the castle is a little bit too stuffy for me. I never know how I'm supposed to act."

I laugh, nodding. "Trust me, that feeling never goes away."

20

MARGOT

LIFE CAN CHANGE directions on a dime.

I went from being a miserable, self-destructive mess, to realizing that I need to change. I spent months trying to work on myself, only to be thrown head-first into a vat of bubbling feelings for a man I hadn't even known existed.

Is it too much to hope for that this thing with Dante could be real?

It's scary to jump into a relationship with Prince Dante. I don't want to get hurt. I want to protect myself, my mental health, and my baby. I want to make the best decision possible for my future, no matter what lies ahead with my disease.

But what if that best decision includes him? What if he can provide a life that I thought only existed in fairy tales?

Dante gives me one last kiss before heading off into Farcliff Castle in search of his brother. Luca is meeting with Prince Damon to talk about the next steps with regard to our safety.

As I walk back to my guest room in the castle, a smile drifts over my face.

For the first time in a long, long time, I feel good. I don't mean a chemical, artificial kind of good. I don't mean a numb kind of good.

I mean truly, deeply happy.

Then, my baby kicks for the first time.

Stopping in the middle of the hallway, joy floods my spirit like I've never felt before. A laugh tumbles out of my mouth as I put both hands to my stomach, feeling the quickening of new life inside me.

Right now, it doesn't matter who the father is. It doesn't matter that my career is hanging on by a thread, or that I'm not sure if things between Dante and I can really work.

Nothing matters, because my baby just moved. I laugh, alone in the hallway, as tears start to fill my eyes. I know that it's not a coincidence that the moment I allowed myself to feel joy, the baby moved.

This baby wants me to be happy. It can feel everything I feel, and it's gone through a tough existence so far. The instant I let myself be really, truly happy, my child let me know that it was right.

That Dante is right.

That what I'm doing is good.

Leaning against the wall, I wrap my arms around myself. My smile practically splits my face in half until the baby stops kicking, and I let out a happy sigh.

That's the only sign that I need to follow Dante to Argyle.

No more hesitation. No more doubts. No more holding back.

I'm jumping head-first into my feelings, because I know that it's the only way for me to move forward.

Pushing myself off the wall, I let my feet carry me back to my bedroom. I don't even remember the walk there. I'm too distracted by the joy exploding inside me like a million fireworks flashing through my soul.

Then, my joy turns to ash when I see a man step out of my bedroom.

I'd recognize him anywhere.

Hunter.

I let out a yelp, stumbling backward. My hands go to my stomach, protecting the life inside me. He's dressed in a castle valet uniform, wearing a sneer on his face. I never realized how ugly he was until I saw this vindictive side of him.

"Margot, Margot, Margot," he starts, taking a step toward me. "How you've betrayed me."

"I haven't done anything, Hunter."

"I created you." Another step closer. "And you turned your back on me."

"You poisoned my sister."

"I tried to give you a chance to come back to me, but you threw it in my face."

"How did you get my medical records? How did you get into the castle?"

He spreads his arms, motioning to the uniform. "It's not hard, when you have the means."

My heart thumps, and for the thousandth time since I fired him, I wonder who Hunter really is. What did he do to get me to the top? How did I earn the acting roles that I was given?

Was my rise to fame done using dirty, underhanded tricks?

"You were always a fucking idiot, Margot," he spits. "And whose bun is baking in there, huh? It wouldn't be Prince Luca's, would it?"

My jaw clenches. I try to back away from him, but my back hits the wall. My fingers clutch the picture rail as my mind speeds, trying to find a way out of this situation. Hunter is stronger than me. He's faster than me. I'll never be able to get away.

Wasn't the castle supposed to be safer than our house?

Then, Hunter's eyes brighten. "Not Luca's. Beckett's, maybe? The timing would make sense. Luca was never interested in you, anyway. Beckett, on the other hand..."

My heart takes off at full speed, bouncing off my ribcage. A lump forms in my throat as my cheeks flush, and Hunter starts to laugh. He throws his head back, laughing louder and louder.

Before he can say anything, though, a body slams into him. I hear an *oof* as the air is knocked out of his lungs. A mess of legs and arms falls to the ground, and I recognize Dante as he grapples with Hunter. The sound of boots rushing down the hallway thump in the distance, but they don't get here before Hunter lands a punch to Dante's face.

I scream, taking a step forward.

"Stay back, Margot!" Dante says, dodging another punch as he lands one to Hunter's midsection.

They kick, scratch, and punch at each other until guards arrive to haul Dante off the intruder. Hunter is dragged away, screaming obscenities in my direction. His eyes are blazing. His gaze sends chills down my spine and all I can do is stay rooted in place, watching him be taken away.

I only realize I'm shivering when Dante puts his arms around me. He rubs his palms over my arms, searching my face.

"Are you okay?"

"I should be asking you that," I say, bringing my fingers up to the bruise already blossoming on his cheekbone. "You're going to get a black eye."

"It's fine," he says, grabbing my hand to kiss my fingertips.

"There's only about two hundred photographers desperate to take my picture."

I laugh shakily, wrapping my arms around my man.

My heart is in my throat. My mouth is dry. All I can do is hang onto Dante and clutch my stomach, fear swirling through my whole body.

My baby doesn't kick.

Dante holds me close until the captain of castle security brings us down to the offices to take our statements. From then on, everything is a whirlwind. It's decided that all four of us—Ivy, Luca, Dante, and I—will go back to Argyle. Farcliff Castle has been breached, and they need to protect the royal family. They'll increase security on the castle, but I get the sense that we're deemed to be security risks.

We pack bags as Dante calls for the jet to be prepared. I call Felicity to let her know, ignoring her protests.

Then, I call Melissa and ask her to come with me. Even though I'm happy with Ivy, Luca, and Dante, I'd still love to have a familiar face with me.

I'm scared. I need a friend.

"Are you kidding me? Of course I want a tropical vacation and a stay at the Argyle Palace," Melissa laughs. "Be at the airport in half an hour."

I let out a relieved sigh. "Thank you."

Hunter is kept in custody, and I hear the guards talking about charging him with trespassing and possibly even treason. They talk about him being locked up for a long, long time.

The thought of him being behind bars makes me sad for the past that we shared, but also relieved. Even going to Argyle doesn't seem like enough distance between me and Hunter.

I'm not allowed back in the guest room. The guards sweep

it for any dangerous substances and explosives, but nothing is found. Hunter says he was only there to try to find information on me and my pregnancy, which he was planning to sell to the tabloids.

I don't know if I believe him. The man who helped launch my career is a stranger to me now.

The world he operated in is one of gossip, media, power, and money. He kept the ugly side of fame away from me, until now. When he tried to poison my sister, everything changed.

Now, it's about to change again.

Luca's face is grim as we board the plane. He keeps a protective arm around Ivy, and a part of me is relieved that they found each other. At least I don't have to worry about Ivy's safety when Luca's around. I don't have to worry about her babies being taken care of.

When Dante's hand slides over my lower back, I let out a sigh.

Is it possible that I've found what Ivy has, too?

But as we board the plane and I take my seat beside Dante, the gremlins in my head laugh, whispering that this is just another heartbreak in the making.

21

DANTE

THE WHOLE POINT of going to Farcliff Castle was that it was supposed to be safer from the paparazzi, but I knew that we'd be more exposed. There are hundreds of staff at the castle, and there's evidently a leak somewhere.

The good news is, now that Hunter is in custody, we don't have to worry about him. The captain of castle security assured us that he'd be locked up for good. It's one less threat we need to worry about.

Still, it feels good to be going home. As I slide my hand into Margot's, I realize that it feels good to be taking her back, too.

I want to show her where I come from. I want to take her to white, sandy beaches and kiss her under the palm trees.

I want to take her out of that toxic, gossip-fueled world that she's used to, and show her the serenity of privacy.

I want to treat her like a princess.

As she leans her head against my shoulder, she lets out a soft sigh. Luca has one arm around Ivy, with the other resting on her belly.

Both sisters' baby bumps are growing.

For the first time, I really think about what that means. Bottles, diapers, vomit, chubby little feet and hands. Crying, giggling, and the wonder in a baby's eyes.

Sleepless nights.

Fatherhood.

I never thought that I'd be a father. I gave up on the idea of sharing my life with anyone a long time ago. For the most part, as soon as women realized that I wasn't going to catapult them into fame and society, they avoided me.

Or maybe I avoided them.

I resigned myself to the fact that I'd spend my days alone. I told myself that I'd be the fun uncle, and I'd take care of my brothers' kids.

Now, there's no doubt in my mind that being a father is what I want—and I want it with Margot. Even if the kid isn't technically mine, it already feels like it is. I care about the child as much as I care about Margot. As the jet takes off, the realization that I love Margot hits me like a bullet to the chest.

I love her.

I love her.

I love her.

Margot shifts, lifting her head up to look at me. "You okay?"

I nod. "I'm great."

We recline our seats, and Margot snuggles into me. The hostess on the plane brings me a fresh ice pack for my face. The doctor cleared me to fly, but warned me that I'd have a nasty bruise. I settle back into my seat and hold Margot close.

Luca glances at me, and a grin spreads over his face. He gives me a slight nod, and then turns his attention back to Ivy.

We found the LeBlanc sisters at the most unlikely of

times, but they complete us in ways we never imagined. It feels good to have Margot—and it feels good to have Luca back, too. For the first time in a long time, I feel like my family is coming back together.

When we arrive at the palace in Argyle, King Theo is waiting for us. He wraps his arms around me and Luca, and then smiles warmly at Ivy and Margot.

In this moment, I'm grateful for Theo's geniality. It's what makes him a good king and a great brother. His smile isn't polite and forced. It's genuine.

I can see Margot relax as soon as he says her name. The palace in Argyle doesn't feel like Farcliff Castle. It doesn't feel like we're hiding away from anything here.

It feels like coming home.

I lead Margot to my bedroom at the far end of the palace. It's tucked away from everyone else—exactly how I used to live. She smiles, leaning her head against my shoulder and letting out a happy sigh.

"I like it here."

"Good," I say, laying a kiss in her blonde hair.

We get into bed and fall asleep right away. For the first time in weeks, it's a deep, peaceful sleep. There's no checking the windows and doors, no security reports to look through at the end of the day, no tossing and turning at every sound.

No nightmares.

Just peace.

Margot wakes up with a smile on her face. She grabs my hand and places it on her stomach, grinning from ear to ear.

My eyes widen. I've never felt a baby kicking before.

"Whoa."

"I know," she laughs. "It's so crazy."

"What does it feel like?"

"Sort of like little flutters." Margot smiles, shaking her head. "I never thought I'd be happy about having a baby like this. I mean, you know, getting pregnant without being married, and with my life being upside down." She takes a deep breath, glancing at me. "But it feels right."

"Is it important to you to be married before the baby comes?"

Margot shrugs. "I thought it was before, but now... I don't know. All that matters is that it's healthy."

A proposal is on the tip of my tongue. I'd marry her today, if she let me. But I know it's not the right time, so I hold back.

Margot stretches her arms above her head, smiling as my eyes drift down her body.

"You make me feel sexy even as my stomach is growing by the day," Margot says. "I like when you look at me like that."

"You are sexy," I answer. "It's easy to look at you like this."

When we make love, it feels different. It feels like we're meant to be here, and meant to be with each other. There are no more barriers between us. By coming with me to Argyle, Margot has shown me that she trusts me and she wants to be with me. By sharing her pregnancy with me, she's telling me that she sees me as a partner.

When we finally get out of bed, Margot walks to the tall French doors that lead out onto my wide balcony. She opens them, inhaling the scent of the sea air. A soft, warm breeze sweeps through the room, and Margot lets out a sigh.

"It's so hot here. It's not even nine o'clock and I'm sweating already."

"You'll get used to it."

"Hope you like sweaty pregnant women, because that's what you're going to get."

"I like you however you are, so I guess that means I like sweaty pregnant women."

Margot laughs, shaking her head. She gathers her thick, long, blonde hair into a messy bun on top of her head and fans herself with a hand. "I might have to chop my hair off."

"And I'd still love you with short hair," I say. It slips out of me so naturally that I don't even realize I've said the 'L' word until Margot's eyes widen.

"You..."

My heart stutters. I push myself up on the pillows, leaning against the headboard. Staring into Margot's eyes, I nod. "I love you, Margot."

The air thickens between us, crackling with energy. Margot stares at me, wordless.

Maybe it's too soon. I mean, hell, of course it's too soon. I've known the woman, what, a month? A bit more?

I don't regret saying it, though. I'd say it a thousand times, because it's the truth. I love Margot LeBlanc. Maybe I've loved her since she mistook me for the pool boy, or since I saw her gather her courage and give a perfect interview after having a panic attack.

I'm not sure when it started, but I know it's the truth.

Margot's bottom lip trembles. "How?"

"What do you mean, how?" I laugh. "I don't know how. I just do."

Margot slides into bed next to me, staring at me with wide eyes.

I grin. "I'll be honest, that wasn't exactly the response I was hoping for when I professed my love to you."

Margot blinks before shaking her head. She grins at me, shrugging. "You said you loved me how I am. Shouldn't that include unexpected reactions?"

"True." I wrap my arms around her and tackle her into

the pillows. "And it was the truth. I love you, Margot."

"You do realize that I'm pregnant, right? I'm going to have a baby? You're ready for that? For a birth? Blood, bodily fluids, maybe even tearing my vagina? Hemorrhoids? It's not pretty. *I* don't even know if I'm ready for it. How can you be ready?"

I can hear the hesitation in her voice, and it makes my chest feel tight. How can I tell her that yes, she's enough? How can I let her know that my love for her extends to the baby? That I see a future with her that I never even imagined would be possible for me?

"I love you, Margot LeBlanc. Pregnant, sweaty, short- or long-haired. However you are, I love you like I never thought was possible." I kiss the tip of her nose. "Even if your vagina tears and you get hemorrhoids."

Margot's eyes mist, and I watch her gulp. She laughs, putting her hands to my face and kissing my lips. "I love you too, Dante. I love you so much it scares the shit out of me."

"What's life without a little healthy fear, though, right?"

"If you say so."

I smile, kissing the woman of my dreams before moving to her growing baby bump and kissing that, too. It's not just her baby anymore—it's mine, too, and I intend to be the best father I can possibly be.

In the very depths of my heart, there's a tremor. A nervousness. A hesitation. I try to ignore it, because it's the part of me that's clinging onto the past and all its simplicity. As Margot lays her head against my chest, I inhale the scent of her hair and I know that whatever challenges are coming our way, it'll be worth it if we're together.

The only problem is that I don't yet know what those challenges are going to be, or how much things are just about to change.

22

MARGOT

MELISSA BLOW-DRIES MY HAIR. She's turned me away from the mirror so I can't see what she's doing, but based on the bundles of extensions lying on the side table, and the mass of hair at my feet, she's chopped off a lot of it.

My hair stylist turns off the blow dryer and smiles at me. "You look flippin' amazing, Margot. You should have done this years ago. It's edgy, sexy, and so completely perfect."

"Turn me around already," I laugh, gripping the edges of the chair.

Melissa spins the chair around, and I gasp. She's chopped my hair off, leaving only a short, chin-length bob. I touch the ends of my hair, running my fingers through the smooth, short strands.

"Holy shit," I breathe. "I can't believe we just did that."

"Play with it! Flick your head around! Do you love it?"

I take a deep breath, turning my head from side to side as a smile spreads across my face. "Yeah," I say, glancing at her in the mirror. "I do, actually."

"You sound like you doubted my abilities."

"Never," I grin. "I just doubted my looks without my hair."

"*Pfft*," Melissa says, waving a hand. "Please. *Farcliff's Sexiest Woman*, remember?"

"Not sure how my brand partners will react. Long, blonde hair was written into a lot of my sponsorship contracts."

"Fuck 'em," Melissa says, wrapping her arms around me. "Live your life, Margot. You deserve it. Wear wigs if you have to. Who cares?"

I smile, glancing at myself in the mirror again. It's only hair. I know it's only hair. But it feels significant. Having long, blonde hair has been my 'look' for my entire life. I've always been the blonde bombshell. That's the image that has made me millions.

And I just chopped it off.

It might just be hair, but getting rid of it makes me feel completely free. Free from Hunter, free from the shackles of Farcliff media, free from the tower of fame where I locked myself for years.

I run my fingers through my hair, marveling at how soft it feels.

"You know," I say, glancing at Melissa, "now I understand Britney Spears in 2007. This is incredible."

Melissa laughs. "Except she did it because of a breakdown, and you're doing it because of a breakthrough."

WHEN DANTE SEES me with short hair, his face breaks into a smile and he throws me over his shoulder. I laugh all the way to the bedroom and then fall into bed with him.

We spend the next week in each other's arms. The weight on my shoulders lifts, and I feel more relaxed than I have in a long time. I hadn't realized how much Hunter's presence looming over me was affecting me, and how much pressure I was feeling in Farcliff.

Now, in this tropical island paradise, I feel free.

On our eighth morning in Argyle, I wake up with a smile on my face. Dante runs his hand over my stomach and lets out a soft sighs.

"You're getting sexier by the day, Margot."

I laugh, shaking my head. "If you say so."

Before we can do anything else, a knock sounds on the door. My eyebrows arch as we both glance at the closed door.

"Who is it?" Dante calls out.

"It's me," my sister's answers.

I slide out of bed and wrap a housecoat around me before opening the door. Ivy has a huge smile on her face. Her pregnancy is much more obvious than mine—either because she has a smaller body or because she's having twins. We're approaching twenty-one weeks, now, and we're both starting to show a little bit more.

"What's going on?" I pull the door open wider.

Ivy glances at Dante in bed, her cheeks flushing. She turns her eyes back to me. "Luca and I are getting married."

My face breaks into a smile as warmth floods through my chest. I throw my arms around my sister. She grunts when I hug her, laughing.

I pull away, taking her left hand in mine and glancing at the rock on her finger. I wiggle my eyebrows, and Ivy laughs.

"My little sister is getting married," I sigh.

She arches her eyebrows at me. "I mean today, Margot. We're getting married today."

"What?"

"I want to be married before the twins come. I know it's old-fashioned, but it just feels right. Waiting to call Luca my husband is torture, so when he brought it up last week, we decided to just go for it."

"Today?" I frown.

Ivy laughs, nodding. "Yeah, today."

My heart thumps as I gulp. I run my fingers through my hair. "What about your friends? Dad? Don't you want to wait so you can plan the wedding? Won't the people of Argyle want some big ceremony?"

Ivy shakes her head. "It doesn't matter. None of that matters. Georgie and Giselle are flying down this morning. They'll be here around noon. Dad left us, Margot. I don't care if he's not here. Luca said the people of Argyle would understand, and we can have a bigger ceremony next year. King Theo has already agreed."

My shock dissolves into joy, and I wrap my arms around my sister again. I laugh, squeezing her tight. When I pull away again, my eyes are full of tears and I shake my head.

"I can't believe this is happening."

"I know."

"I'm happy for you."

"I was wondering..."—Ivy bites her lip—"...if you'd be my maid of honor?"

My heart skips a beat. A lump forms in my throat, and my chest grows tighter. I swallow thickly. "Really?"

"Yeah," my sister smiles.

"Even after everything that happened? I don't know if I deserve it, Ivy. What about Georgie or Giselle?"

Ivy takes my hands in hers and gives them a squeeze. "Margot, you've done so much for me. You provided for our whole family growing up, and you gave me a platform from which to launch my business. You did the hardest thing in the world by going to therapy and changing your life, and you've withstood all the horrible things in the media. You're my sister, Margot," Ivy says. "Of course you deserve it."

Tears sting my eyes, and I shake my head. I don't feel like I deserve to be by my sister's side. It's because of me that she was in the hospital. I kept her as my personal assistant for years, not thinking that she might want to do something different.

Ivy reads my mind. "Margot, stop blaming yourself for things that aren't your fault."

"I held you back for so long, Ivy."

She laughs, kindness emanating from her like a bright light. "You never held me back from anything. I was just too chicken to go out and grab it. Once I did, you had a little wobble as you got used to it, and then you were the most supportive person in the world. I love you, Margot."

Tears are streaming down my face now, and Ivy hugs me again. She squeezes her arms around me so tight I can't move, and I let my tears soak into the fabric of her shirt.

"Would you be willing to walk me down the aisle?" Ivy asks.

My eyebrows jump. "Me?"

"I sent word to Father about the wedding, but he's been sailing for so long, I'm not sure if it'll reach him in time. Plus, you've been more of a parent to me than he has for many years now. I don't love the idea of a man handing me off to another man like I'm some horse he bought at a fair. I'd much rather have my sister, role model, and closest friend walk me toward the love of my life so we can join our families together."

I smile, shaking my head. "Only you could make a nice, old tradition seem so patriarchal and wrong."

"What's a tradition if it doesn't mean anything to you? I want my wedding to mean something to *me*. Having you by my side is a big part of that."

Emotion chokes my throat. To think that Ivy cares so much about me that she wants me to walk her down the aisle means more than I can say. I thought I'd lost my sister. That we'd drifted apart. That she thought of me as a self-centered, vapid celebrity.

But she doesn't. I'm her sister, and she's by my side —forever.

I'm not alone at all. I have so many people around me that care.

I nod, wrapping my arms around her once more. "I'd love to."

I feel another hand on my back and look up to see Dante. He's wearing nothing but boxer shorts, but somehow, it doesn't matter. He hugs Ivy, pulling away with a smile.

"Welcome to the family, Ivy."

Ivy smiles wider. She nods. "Thanks. Take care of my sister, Your Highness."

"I intend to." The Prince slides his arm around my shoulders. I lean into him, letting the tension in my chest ease. Ivy slips out of the door and leaves us alone again.

I release a sigh, wrapping my arms around Dante. He holds me tight, laying a soft kiss in my short hair.

"You okay?" he asks softly.

I nod. "Yeah. I'm happy for her. I just wasn't expecting it all to happen so fast, but I guess it makes sense."

The Prince pulls away, staring into my eyes. They're bright and clear, but unreadable. He parts his lips, sliding his tongue out to moisten them, but says nothing.

As we stand there, I can't help but wonder if he wants to be my husband, and if he, too, is wondering how long it'll take the two of us to reach that point.

If we ever will.

I slide my arms around his neck, and the Prince leans his forehead against mine. Closing my eyes, I soak up the love that shines from him. He makes me stronger.

In that moment, I realize that I need to tell him the truth

about the baby's father and about my illness. I need to tell Ivy, too, and I need to do it soon.

I'm sick of having secrets. Sick of carrying them on my own. Sick of holding myself back from true happiness with Dante.

Most of all, I'm sick of wondering if he'll still be there for me if he knows the truth about the baby, and about my Huntington's disease diagnosis.

It's my illness that worries me. How can I expect a man to accept me like this? How can I expect him to agree to be with me...and how can I ask him to stick by my side? Being with me means agreeing to a life as a caretaker. It means seeing me deteriorate, and watching my personality change. It means watching me die early.

Doesn't he deserve better?

When the Prince presses his lips to mine, it feels like he hears my thoughts. It's like he can sense a shift inside me, and he's telling me opening up to him is the right thing to do.

I have to tell them the truth, and I will—after the wedding.

Today is Ivy's day.

Tomorrow, I tell Dante the truth.

23

IVY

MARGOT, Giselle, and Georgie are staring at me, eyes misty, hands clasped to their chests, smiles splitting their faces open. My heart is overflowing.

"You look incredible, Ivy," Georgie says, shaking her head. "I can't believe you're getting married."

"I know," I smile, glancing in the mirror. Melissa touches up my hair one last time, her eyes full of tears.

I take a deep breath. "Everything has happened so fast, but it feels right."

Margot takes a step toward me and squeezes her hands on my shoulders. "I'd hug you, but I don't want to mess up your hair and makeup." Her bottom lip trembles, and she shakes her head. "I'm going to start crying."

"Thank you for being here." I glance at the twins. "All of you."

"Of course," Giselle says, slinging her arm around her twin. "We wouldn't miss it for anything in the world."

"How's everything at the bakery? Your brothers will be okay for a few days on their own?" I ask.

"Stop thinking about work," Georgie replies, laughing.

"It's your wedding day. Everything at the bakery is fine. Irving is there full-time, and you know he's been managing restaurants his whole life."

I nod, taking a deep breath. A soft knock on the door makes us turn our heads, and my father pokes his head through the door.

"Dad!" My eyebrows jump up.

Margot stiffens.

"Hi, honey," he says, stepping through the door.

"I didn't know if you'd gotten our invitation. I thought you were still at sea."

"Cut my sailing trip short," he says. "I couldn't miss my daughter's wedding!" My father wraps me in a hug, obviously not worried about my hair and makeup.

He turns to Margot, nodding. "Hello."

"Hi, Dad." They hug each other awkwardly, and my heart sinks.

We haven't spoken to our father very often since he left Farcliff. Once Margot made enough money after Mama died, he took off on his own. I sent an invitation to him for the wedding, but I didn't even hear a response. I assumed he hadn't gotten it.

He must have been close to Argyle to make it here on such short notice.

Margot and I haven't talked about our father very often, but I think she resents him leaving. As Margot and I grew closer to each other through our pregnancies and everything that has happened in the last few months, I've realized just how isolated my sister was. I thought her life was a dream, but I'm starting to think she's been deeply unhappy for a long, long time.

None of us realized. Maybe none of us cared.

"I'm proud of you, Ivy. I always thought Margot would be the one to marry well." My father smiles at me.

Margot makes a noise, covering it up with a cough.

I nod. "Okay, well, I think it's time for us to go down."

My father extends his arm toward me, smiling. "I guess I'll be walking you down the aisle," he grins.

Margot's face falls. My chest tightens, and for a moment, the air in the room is heavy. My father looks at me expectantly, nodding to his outstretched arm. Margot drops her chin to her chest, staring at the floor.

I take a deep breath. "Actually, Dad, Margot is going to walk me down the aisle."

"What?" both Margot and my father ask in unison. My father looks confused, and Margot's eyes are wide.

I nod. "It's what I want."

Margot's bottom lip trembles, her eyes speaking volumes. Her chest heaves with every breath, and I know I've made the right decision.

My sister means the world to me, and she's sacrificed so much to provide for my father and me. It's only in the past couple of months, when the media scrutiny has turned to me, that I've realized what she deals with every single day. Sharing that experience has brought us so much closer together, and I want to show her how much I care.

"Why?" Dad asks, frowning. "Don't you want a traditional wedding?"

I laugh, running my hand over my stomach. "There's absolutely nothing traditional about my wedding." I hook my arm into Margot's, patting my father's shoulder with my other hand. "Come on, Dad. I'll get the staff to set up a seat for you in the front row."

Our little group follows a valet down to the palace gardens, where chairs have been set up near the gazebo. A tall fountain sprays in the background, and the azure waters of the Caribbean sparkle beyond. There are white flowers absolutely everywhere, draped on every chair and every surface of the gazebo.

Luca and his brothers are standing at the end of the aisle, and my heart jumps in my chest. I watch the twins walk down the aisle, followed by my father, and finally me.

Prince Luca's eyes lift to mine, and everything inside me cries out with joy. Margot squeezes my arm in hers as tears threaten to spill down my cheeks.

A few months ago, I was directionless, scared, and lonely.

Now, I've gained a husband, two children, and a real relationship with my sister—not to mention my dream business.

Luca's eyes shine as he watches me make my slow walk down the aisle. By the time I get to him, Margot is crying. She kisses my cheek and takes her spot on the gazebo beside me, but I hardly see her at all.

I only have eyes for Luca.

My soon-to-be husband is wearing a perfectly tailored suit. His top button is undone, and he's not wearing a tie.

"You look amazing, babe," he whispers, his eyes sweeping over my body.

"What? This old thing?" I say, fluffing the full, white skirt of my exquisite dress, sourced by the castle stylist overnight.

Luca laughs, shaking his head. "I'm the luckiest man in the world."

"You sure are," Margot says behind me. The small crowd of friends and family laughs, and the officiant starts the ceremony.

I don't hear a word. The warm breeze flows through my hair, carrying the scent of the ocean and beaches toward us. The only thing I see is Luca. In his eyes, I see bottomless love.

I see a future I never could have imagined, and I see my true home.

As soon as I hear the words 'husband and wife,' Luca sweeps his arms around me and crushes his lips to mine. I laugh, kissing him back with the ferocity of my love for him. He drops to his knees, pressing his lips to my growing belly before resting his forehead against it.

Tears stream down my face. My makeup is probably ruined, but it doesn't matter.

I throw one last glance toward Margot and the twins before wrapping my arm around Luca's waist and letting him lead me back down the aisle.

I'm married.

We head to one of the large reception rooms in the castle. How the staff managed to rustle up perfect decorations in such a short amount of time is beyond me. The whole room is immaculate, with flowers and lights and fabric draped everywhere. It looks like a fairy tale, and I feel like a princess.

I guess once the King makes it official in writing, I *will* be a princess.

We dance, and eat, and laugh. I stay on Luca's arm until the sun goes down, kissing him every chance I get.

For that day, we forget about Beckett. We forget about Hunter. We forget about everything that happened in Farcliff, and we just celebrate love.

My father doesn't seem too upset about not walking me down the aisle, and he drinks himself to an early bedtime. I even see him laughing with Margot and dancing with one of the waitresses.

For one day, everything is perfect.

"My feet are so sore," I sigh, resting my head on Luca's shoulder. We're sitting at the table after having devoured our wedding cake, watching our guests dance and drink.

"Bedtime, then," Luca says.

I yelp when he picks me up, hooking my arms around his shoulders.

"I'm taking my bride to bed," Luca announces to no one in particular. King Theo and Queen Cara smile, leaning their heads against each other as they watch us walk out. I rest my head on Luca's chest, listening to his heartbeat as he carries me to our wedding bed.

When he lays me down on the soft pillows and kisses my lips, I let out a soft sigh.

"I didn't know it was possible to be this happy," I say.

"Me, neither." Luca's eyes shine, and he presses his lips to mine again. "You complete me, Poison."

"I love you, husband." I smile, shaking my head. "It feels good to say that. Husband. Hubby. Life partner. Love of my life."

"Mother of my children," Luca completes, wrapping his arms around me.

He undresses me slowly, kissing every inch of skin that is exposed. We make love that night, worrying about nothing and no one except each other.

My wedding is perfect, from morning until night.

But all good things come to an end, and I don't realize how quickly my happiness will come crashing down.

24

DANTE

THE MORNING AFTER THE WEDDING, I wake up hungover as hell. I didn't even think I drank that much, but the atmosphere must have gotten the better of me. Celebrating with my brother and Ivy was the most fun I've had in a long, long time.

Now, though, my head is pounding and my mouth tastes like stale alcohol and bad decisions.

I groan, turning over to see Margot sitting at the desk in the corner of the room. She types a few things on her laptop before turning the chair to glance at me.

She arches an eyebrow, grinning. "Feeling fresh?"

"Not as fresh as you, obviously."

"I got you some water and ibuprofen. It's on the nightstand."

"You're a treasure." I swallow the pills and half the glass of water before laying back down in bed. Exhaling, I stare at the ceiling.

"One good thing about being pregnant is not drinking." Margot laughs, climbing into bed beside me. "Which means no hangovers."

"Why did you let me drink that much?"

"I'm not the boss of you, Your Highness."

"At least I had fun...from what I can remember."

Margot giggles, laying a kiss on my cheek. "Why don't you go for a dip in the ocean? I used to love getting in the pool after a big night. You'll feel better after."

I nod, turning to stare at Margot. Somehow, when she cut her hair, it made her features stand out even more. Her eyes look like jewels. Her lips are lush. Her cheekbones are regal. It's like without the long waves always framing her face, I can see her all the more clearly.

She's incredible.

"You're probably right," I sigh. "Maybe a swim would help. You want to join?"

Margot shakes her head. "I have a few things to finish up for work. Felicity wants me to review a bunch of statements she's putting out about the Hunter situation."

I nod before pushing myself up to sit. Groaning, I clutch my head when it starts pounding. Margot rubs my back, and I let out a sigh.

I grimace "Okay, well, I'll be back soon. You have a doctor's appointment today, yes?"

Margot nods, a shadow passing over her face. "Yeah."

I take a deep breath. "Can I... Can I come?" I didn't mean for my voice to squeak so much on the last word, and I clear my throat to cover it up.

Going to her doctor's appointment with her would feel like a big step. From now on, we'd be doing this together, as partners.

But Margot hesitates. Her brows draw together, and my heart starts to thud. She doesn't have to say yes. It's her right to go to the doctor on her own. Maybe we aren't as close as I thought we were. After all, it's her baby and her body.

Then, Margot takes a deep breath and drags her eyes up to mine. She nods. "Yeah. I'd like you to."

"Are you sure? Because it looks like you're in physical pain at the thought of me coming with you."

Margot laughs, and the lines on her forehead disappear. She shakes her head. "I'm just not used to having someone by my side."

Laying a soft kiss on her forehead, I leave her to her work and head to the bathroom to brush my teeth. I avoid looking at the haggard, hungover face that stares back at me in the mirror, choosing instead to take Margot's advice and let the ocean cleanse me of last night's overindulgence.

It's still early, but the palace staff is already up and awake. Grabbing a towel from one of the pool attendants, I hook it over my arm and head toward the private beach near the palace.

"Sir," the attendant says as I walk away, "would you like me to accompany you?"

I shake my head. "No, thank you."

"But the King has ordered that—"

"I'm just going for a swim," I answer, forcing a smile. My head pounds. "It's a private beach, enclosed in the royal grounds. I'll be fine."

The pool attendant shifts his weight from foot to foot, finally nodding reluctantly.

I walk a short way over a berm to my favorite place in the entire world—the Argyle Royal Bay. It's a sheltered beach, with tall palm trees lining a white, sandy shore. A warm breeze blows through the trees and I inhale deeply, ready for the ocean to cleanse the cobwebs from my mind.

When my toes touch the water, I jump back. It's colder than I expected.

Taking a deep breath, I set my jaw. Then, I sprint. I crash

into the water, diving down below the surface. The cool water shocks my senses. I'm alive. I laugh, breaking the surface of the water and diving back down again.

By the time I walk back out of the surf, I feel fresh, clean, and alive. The last remnants of last night's drinks are washed away, and I'm ready for some food.

Life is good.

I have a woman that I love, a baby on the way, and my family is happy.

When I reach my towel and shake the sand off it, movement catches my eye on the edge of the beach.

Beckett steps out from behind a palm tree. My heart stutters, and my hands ball into fists. I drop the towel, widening my stance and setting my jaw.

"Beckett."

"Your Highness," he drawls, walking toward me.

"What are you doing here?" I scan the beach, wishing I hadn't said no to the pool attendant. "We've been looking for you for months."

Beckett barks out a laugh. "It's been entertaining to watch you fail."

"What do you want?"

"I see Luca's married," he says, narrowing his eyes. My heart thumps. Last night was a private ceremony. No one in the public knows about it yet.

Beckett must have eyes inside the palace.

I nod, trying not to let my fear show. "Yes, he is."

"And you seem to be cozy with Margot LeBlanc." He spits her name out, his lips twitching into a snarl.

Blood pumps through my veins as I stare at my half-brother. There's a strange mixture of anger and sadness inside me.

Anger, because Beckett has caused immeasurable levels

of pain for our family.

Sadness, because Beckett was my brother.

I didn't care that we didn't share the same father. He was my brother. We grew up together. Played together. Became men together.

He has always been my brother.

Just like Margot's child is my child.

Beckett kicks his foot in the sand, sending a spray of it toward me. "How does it feel to have both Luca's and my sloppy seconds?"

I freeze, staring at Beckett. My mouth turns dry. I clear my throat, trying to dislodge the rocks that have taken up residence at the base of my throat.

"What are you talking about?"

"Oh, she didn't tell you?" Becket's eyes glint. "Margot and me..." He trails off, arching an eyebrow.

"Margot and you, what?"

Beckett's mouth curls into an ugly grin. "You haven't put two and two together, have you? To be honest, I'm not surprised she would choose you as a partner. Makes it easier to keep it in the family."

"What the fuck are you talking about?" My heart is hammering, my ribs barely able to keep it contained.

"You know what I'm talking about, Dante."

"I don't." I'm being strangled. I can't speak, or breathe, or do anything except stand here and stare at the man I once called my brother.

"The baby is mine. I guess even after I stuck a needle in her, she was strong enough to stay alive and to keep the baby. Surprising, to be honest." He stares at his nails, feigning disinterest. "I thought she was going to die."

The words hit me like bullets, knocking me back as they

pierce my body. Wheezing as I inhale, I stumble back. "What?"

"Margot always seemed like a crafty woman. Smart." Beckett grins, lifting his eyes up to mine. "I guess since she couldn't be with me or Luca, she chose the next best thing."

"You're lying."

"Am I?" He arches an eyebrow, his steely eyes trained on me.

"It's not true. You're just trying to break this family apart. You couldn't get to Luca, you couldn't have Cara, so now you're going after me."

Beckett shrugs, his eyes still staring into mine. "Ask her."

"Why should I?"

"Because you already know it's true."

If I was in my right mind, I would chase after my half-brother. I'd tackle him to the ground and call for help. I'd knock him out and drag him back to the palace.

I'd be a hero.

Instead, I just stand there, mouth agape, watching him walk away.

In one, quick revelation, Beckett has made my entire world crash around me.

If the baby is Beckett's, then it makes sense that Margot wouldn't want to reveal it. Maybe Beckett is right, and she's just been using me for my title. She couldn't have Luca, because he wasn't interested. She couldn't have Beckett, because he betrayed us.

So, she chose me.

Lucky last.

She did exactly what my mother did, jumping from one brother to the next. Getting knocked up and not caring about the consequences.

I shake my head. It can't be true. She told me she loved

me. I saw it in her eyes. It's real. Our love is real. Our connection is true.

But—she's a world-renown actress. She could have been faking the whole thing.

My mind whirls, bouncing from one idea to the next. Back and forth, I move between trusting Margot and hating that she's used me.

Stumbling across the beach, I lose my footing and fall to my knees. Sand clings to my damp legs, covering my body as I stand up again. Staring at myself, I frown. I drag my feet all the way back to the palace, ignoring the pool attendant.

Once I get inside the castle, all my senses jolt back to reality. I rush through the hallways toward the main dining room, where I know Theo will be.

He looks up when I burst through the door. "Beckett's here. He came up to me at the beach."

Theo's chair clatters to the floor as he stands up. With one wave of the hand, he sends guards rushing down the hallway.

Between gulping breaths, I tell him where I saw Beckett.

I don't tell him about the revelation. I don't tell him about the baby. I don't tell him that my heart is breaking.

For that, I need to see Margot.

In a haze, I stumble out of the dining room and down the hallway toward my chambers. Toward Margot.

Toward the truth.

25

MARGOT

DANTE'S EYES are blazing when he storms through the door. He stands in the middle of the room, staring at me. His chest heaves and his hands clench and unclench, over and over again.

He doesn't have to say a word.

He knows.

My heart shatters slowly, bit by bit. One piece at a time, it crumbles in my chest, because I know whatever happened between Dante and me is over.

I stand slowly, forcing myself to drag my eyes up to his. My lip trembles, and I will it to stop. I bite the inside of my cheek until I taste blood, waiting for him to speak.

"Is it true?"

"Is what true?" I ask, already knowing what he means.

"Is Beckett the father?"

In that moment, my world ends. Once again, I was too much of a coward to tell him the truth. He could take the revelation of my pregnancy and tell me that he'd be by my side, but he can't take this.

Why would he?

The air between us thickens. I can't move. A weight settles on my chest, and I find it hard to take a full breath.

My baby, which had been kicking merrily all morning, is still. Waiting. Listening.

Dipping my chin down ever so slightly, I nod. "Yes."

Prince Dante's face crumples, and the sight of his anguish pierces me like a spear to the chest. My heart bleeds, emptying itself of all the hope and happiness that had started to seep in.

I don't cry. I don't speak. I don't tremble.

I just stand there.

Dante roughs a hand through his hair, his eyes bugging out of his head. He stares at the carpet at his feet, mumbling to himself before looking back up at me.

"Why?" he whispers.

I don't know how to answer. Even if I knew what he wanted me to say, I don't know that I could ever speak. How can I explain how much I've suffered? What words could possibly convey the guilt that I've felt over the one night I spent with Beckett?

I drop my eyes.

"Look at me," Dante growls.

Taking a deep breath, I squeeze my eyes shut for a moment before dragging them up to his.

"*Why?*"

"I was lonely," I answer lamely. "Beckett was there. I..." I can't tell him about the diagnosis. It would sound like I was making an excuse.

Dante's lip trembles. "Why didn't you tell me?"

"Because I knew you'd hate me for it."

The Prince's face twists, and I watch the anger mount inside him. He roars, the sound rattling my bones. I sob, clapping a hand over my mouth. Prince Dante spins on his heels, driving his fist into the wall. I flinch as the plaster crumbles, leaving a fist-sized hole in the wall.

The first tear falls from my eye. I clutch my stomach, turning away from him.

"You used me," he says to my back.

I shake my head. "Never."

"You wormed your way into my heart so that your baby would have a father."

I sob. "No. That's not what happened."

"You tried to have Luca, and then Beckett, and finally settled for me. I never meant anything to you."

"*No!*"

His words lash my back like an angry whip, leaving long, bloody welts across my body. I clutch the edge of the desk, raking a breath in through gritted teeth.

"I love you," I whisper, not able to look at him. "I've loved you since the first day we met."

"I don't believe you."

I turn to look at him again, and immediately wish I didn't. Dante's eyes are dead. Empty.

Angry.

The Prince jerks his head to the door. I stuff my laptop and a few things into my purse, rushing out of the room. My feet take me to Ivy's room, but I can't bring myself to knock.

I can hear her and Luca making love on the other side of the door.

She's happy.

Why would I bring my cursed existence into their life? They'll be leaving on a honeymoon soon. Turning on my heels, I find the twins. They're already packed up and ready to go back to Farcliff.

When Giselle sees me, she drops her suitcase and wraps her arms around me.

"What's wrong?"

"I'm coming with you," I say between sobs.

"To Farcliff?"

I nod.

Giselle and Georgina exchange a glance, and then hook their arms into mine and take me to the plane. No one questions me. No one asks me where my suitcase is, or why Dante isn't with me.

It's like everyone knows that something has shifted.

They all know it's over.

The plane ride back to Farcliff is excruciating. Every inch that takes me farther away from Dante feels like my heart is being ripped from my chest. I clutch my hands to my stomach, doubling over in my seat as I wait for the agony to end.

Maybe I should have stayed. Maybe I should have worked it out. Explained. Reassured. Trusted.

What's the point, though?

I saw Dante's eyes.

It's over.

I'm on my own, just like I always thought I would be.

When the flight attendant hands me a glass of sparkling water, I stare at the bubbles that cling to the edge of the glass, tapping them with a fingernail to dislodge them. They rush to the surface and burst.

Georgina slides her hand over my arm and gives me a sympathetic smile. "You want to talk about it?"

"Not really."

She sighs, turning to look forward. Her hand stays on my arm, and I draw a small bit of comfort from the touch.

"You're not alone, you know," she finally says. "We care about you, just like we care about Ivy."

I laugh-snort, shaking my head. "You don't know anything about me," I answer bitterly. "I've always been alone."

Georgie sighs.

I force myself to look at her. "Prince Beckett is the father of my child." The words burn as they come out. Words that I thought I'd never speak out loud. Words that have ruined my relationship and any chance at happiness.

Words that I should have had the courage to say months ago, and all this would have been avoided.

Georgie's eyes widen. "What?"

I chuckle bitterly. "You still think everything will work out, and that I won't end up alone?" I shake my head, staring out the plane window at the endless puffy, white clouds. "I can't come back from this. My agent is in jail for treason, and the father of my child tried to murder a prince. What does that say about me?"

"Um, that you have terrible taste in men?"

I laugh, glancing at Georgie. Her blue braids hang on either shoulder and a kind smile stretches across her lips.

"Come on," she says softly. "You have Ivy. You have us. You have a house and a lot of adoring fans. You have your health. Who cares about the father of your kid? It doesn't mean you're a bad person. It means you made one bad decision. Everyone does that once in a while."

I try to smile, but it comes out as a grimace. I know she's trying to be nice, and I appreciate it.

But she's wrong.

I don't have Ivy. I never did. Ivy is her own person, and best thing I can do for her is to let her live her own life. I saw how happy she was at the wedding. She doesn't need me bringing her down.

I don't have the twins, either. They aren't my friends.

A house? More like a prison.

Adoring fans? More like vultures.

And my health. Well, that's another bombshell that hasn't

dropped yet. But what's the point of telling it now? Who cares if I have Huntington's? I don't want Dante's pity. He's already retracted his love and his commitment to my child. My medical history doesn't change that.

No, it's just me, and my baby.

The way it's always been.

The way it'll always be.

26

DANTE

YOU KNOW the sounds that the adults in the *Charlie Brown Show* make? That's what I hear when Theo debriefs me on the Beckett situation.

Luca is pacing the study, running his hands through his hair over and over again.

But all I can think of is Margot.

She's gone—because of me.

I don't know why I'm surprised. I wanted her to leave. I could hardly stand to look at her when she confirmed that Beckett's the father.

Now that she's gone, it hurts. I regret speaking to her that way. I feel sorry for how we left it.

Worst of all, one of the things that Beckett said plays on repeat in my mind.

Even after I stuck a needle in her, she was strong enough to stay alive.

Beckett caused her overdose. He didn't just try to kill Luca, he tried to kill Margot, too.

But I'm still angry. Heat clutches my heart, squeezing it a

little too hard. Pain slices across my chest, sending daggers of fire up into my throat.

She should be here.

But she lied.

Back and forth, my mind tugs at me. I can't ignore the love I have for her, but I can't get over the fact that she kept the truth from me.

It was a lie by omission, but it was a lie nonetheless. For weeks, we worked on keeping her safe from Beckett. I changed my plans and exposed my face to the media for her sake. I worked to keep her protected from him, and she never told me.

She never had the courage to say who the father was.

I should have known.

It's hard to reconcile my thoughts about Margot. On one hand, I admire her strength and perseverance. She has more resilience than anyone else I know.

On the other hand, she lied. She was weak. She fell into my arms, asking me to care for and protect a baby created by the man who tried to kill Luca.

"Did he say anything about his plans, Dante?" Theo's eyes are sharp as he stares at me, leaning his fists on his desk.

I clear my throat, shaking my head. "No."

"What did he want?" Luca stops pacing, staring at me. "If he didn't threaten me or you again, and he didn't tell you what his plans were, what *did* he want? Why did he talk to you?"

My brothers stare at me as bitterness coats my tongue. I try to swallow the acrid taste in my mouth, but it burns my throat on the way down.

With a deep breath, I resign myself to the pain of speaking the words that hurt so much to hear. "He wanted me to know that he's the father of Margot's child."

Silence.

"W-What?" Luca stares at me, his brows tugging toward each other.

I nod. "Yeah."

"That can't be true."

"I asked her."

"Get her in here," Theo says, glancing at the door. "We need to figure this out."

"She's gone." My voice is completely flat. I stare at a spot on the wall, seeing nothing.

"What do you mean she's gone? She's with Beckett?"

"No." I snap out of my stupor, glancing at Theo. "She left with the twins this morning to go back to Farcliff. We broke up. I guess… I guess she didn't feel like she could stay here."

Luca sucks a breath in, slumping down into a chair. "That complicates things."

I snort bitterly.

The three of us are silent for a moment, until Theo raps his knuckles on his desk. "We need to get Margot back here. She's carrying Argyle royalty, and she shouldn't be on her own in Farcliff. We need to protect her."

I frown, staring at the King. Shame curls in the pit of my stomach as I realize that he's right…

…but I still can't bring myself to agree with him.

I know that no matter what Beckett has done, Margot's baby should be part of our family. That's especially true now that Luca and Ivy are married. We can't leave her out in the cold to fend for herself.

We accepted Beckett as our brother, even though he never believed it. Margot's child is part of this family, too.

Yet, I can't bring myself to say it out loud. Whenever I open my mouth, the only thing that wants to come out is bitterness and anger.

Why couldn't she have just told me the truth? Why did she have to hide this from me?

It makes me wonder what else she's hiding, and why she hid it in the first place. Beckett's words echo in my mind.

Margot always seemed like a crafty woman. I guess since she couldn't be with me or Luca, she chose the next best thing.

His voice plays in my head like a broken record, pushing out any virtuous thoughts that might have taken hold. I can't trust her. I can't believe her. She was just using me.

It feels like I'm a child all over again, confused as to why my mother has left. Mad at her for abandoning us. Mad at her for cheating on my father and lying.

"...So, will you? Dante?" Theo is staring at me, eyebrows arched. Luca's staring at me, too, and I try to straighten up in my chair.

I clear my throat. "Sorry, what was that?"

"Will you go to Farcliff to get Margot back here? She can't be on her own over there. We need to keep her safe."

I shake my head, and my brothers frown at me. "I can't." It comes out as a hoarse whisper, and shame makes my cheeks burn.

"What?" Luca grunts, leaning toward me.

"I can't," I repeat.

"Why not?"

"I can't. I'm sorry." I push myself out of my chair and stumble out of the room.

Making my way back to my own chambers, I grimace when I see Margot's things still strewn around the bedroom. She was in such a hurry to get away from me that she didn't even take her belongings.

Throwing open her suitcase, I start flinging her stuff into it. I scoop all her toiletries into a plastic bag and chuck them into the suitcase. I don't bother folding her clothes. I just crumple them up and toss them in.

How can my brothers not understand how I feel? How could they ask me to go fetch her back to Argyle?

How can they trust her?

Margot lied to us. All of us. She was closer to Beckett than we thought, and she kept it hidden from everyone. She hated the fact that Ivy started a business, and her agent tried to poison her sister.

How can we be sure that she had nothing to do with that? She's at the center of everything bad that's happened to us!

I repeat the words to myself, mumbling angrily as I pack her things away. When I zip the suitcase up and lift it onto its wheels, I'm sweaty and panting. I take a step back, staring at the black bag as if it'll start talking to me.

Huffing, I call a valet into my room and tell him to send the suitcase back to Farcliff. Storming out of my bedroom, I make my way outside. I need some air. I need a drink. I need *something*.

I wander through the palace grounds, but everything reminds me of Margot.

Her laugh. Her smell. Her touch.

I've lost everything that I never even knew I wanted. She promised me a life that I thought was out of reach. I thought I'd be a father, a husband, a good, honest man.

Now? Now, I'm right back to where I started.

The clicking of a camera shutter sends fear spiking through my veins. I glance up to see a reporter hiding behind a tree, seconds before a bodyguard pulls him to the ground and puts him in a headlock.

My eyebrows arch in surprise. I hadn't even realized the bodyguard was behind me, but I vaguely remember Theo saying something about needing to be accompanied everywhere.

The photographer is hauled away, and my heart sinks.

This is my life now. I've exposed my face to the media. I've come out of hiding, and now the public only wants more.

I gave everything up for Margot—including my privacy—and she fucking *lied.*

Lied, lied, lied.

My veins feel like they're full of fire, burning me from the inside out. I can't move without painful heat shooting through my body. I can't breathe without feeling like my lungs are being crushed. I can't speak without scraping razor blades over my vocal cords.

The sounds of the photographer's protests fade as he's hauled away by security, and I still stand in the woods.

Alone.

Tilting my chin up to look at the treetops, a bitter laugh escapes my lips. I used to love being alone. Being by myself was the sweetest joy. Loneliness didn't exist in my life. Solitude was a gift.

Now, everything is soured.

I'm completely, utterly alone...

...and I hate it.

27

MARGOT

"Don't worry about him," Melissa says as she conditions my hair. "Men are dogs."

"Prince Dante isn't a dog."

"Number one, he agreed to be there for you and to take care of your child, even though it wasn't his. Then, he turned around and kicked you out. *Ergo de facto*, he's a dog."

"I didn't know you knew Latin," I say, too tired to smile.

"Carpe diem, baby," Melissa responds, rinsing the conditioner out of my short hair.

She moves me to a chair and blow-dries it. I stare in the mirror at my shortened locks, and bitterness fills my heart.

I chopped my hair off in an impulsive moment, thinking I was turning a leaf. I thought my life was changing for the better.

All I've done is give myself visible proof that I'm a fool.

"There," Mel says, turning the blow drier off. "Bangin'."

"Thanks." I smile sadly, touching the ends of my hair. "Is it bad that I kind of miss the long hair?"

"You're just saying that because your boyfriend is an ass."

"He's not an ass," I shoot back. "And he's not my boyfriend."

"Mark my words, Margot," Melissa says, pointing a comb at me. "He's going to come crawling back."

My chest squeezes. "I'm not sure about that."

"Mark. My. Words." She nods to the door. "Come on. Let's have some food."

"Thanks for coming back so quickly. I know you wanted to visit more of Argyle."

"I couldn't leave you here on your own," Melissa says, wrapping me in a hug.

Following my friend downstairs, I make my way to the kitchen, where my personal chef has prepared a feast. I smile and thank him before grabbing a plateful of food. Mel and I sit down on the living room floor, eating at the coffee table.

We used to do this together when we first met, before I had a mansion with a dining room and fancy chairs. Somehow, it became our tradition. Eating on the floor with Mel is one of the few things that makes me feel normal.

I fold my legs underneath me and put a hand to my stomach. Soon, I'll have to sit at the table. Getting up and down off the floor is becoming more difficult.

I push the food around the plate.

I'm empty. Life is meaningless. It's hard to shake the dread that's growing inside me, and the feeling like there's no use in even trying.

I shake the feeling away—or at least, I try to. It clings to me like a bad smell, sending nausea spiking through my stomach.

Then, as if responding to the sensation, my baby kicks me right in the ribs.

I grunt, doubling over.

"What?" Melissa says, dropping her fork. "You okay?"

The baby kicks me again, harder. I wince, nodding. "I'm fine. I think my kid is trying to tell me to get it together."

"I like your baby already."

I smile, grimacing. Patting my stomach, I brace myself as another kick lands. Pressing softly at my stomach, I try to encourage my baby to move away.

The baby lands one last kick, and then stops moving. I sigh in relief.

"I don't think I'll ever get used to that."

Melissa grins, and I turn to my plate again. I force myself to eat a few bites, and the nausea inside me settles. Laying a hand on my pregnant stomach, I sigh.

Once again, my child has saved me. Anytime I falter, he or she gives me strength—even in the form of sharp kicks to the ribs.

As I finish my food, I scoot back on the floor and lean my back against the couch.

"Chin up, Margot," Melissa says, grabbing an unfinished bite off my plate. "It'll be okay."

"I guess it was too much to expect that the Prince would agree to take care of my unborn child." I smile sadly. "It was fun while it lasted."

"Look, Margot, you need to realize that you don't need him. You don't need anyone." Mel stares at me, stretching her legs out and leaning back against her elbows. "You're honestly the strongest person I've ever met. You've been the sole breadwinner for your family since you were a preteen. You watched your mother get sick and die. You watched your father leave once you made enough money for him to retire, and you fired your agent when you found out he was a horrible person. You faltered, sure, but you got yourself some help and are now pulling yourself together. You found out you were pregnant and took it in stride."

I shake my head. "I feel the exact opposite of strong. A gust of wind could send me into a mental breakdown."

"You and me both," Mel grins. "But seriously, Margot, you need to start feeling proud of yourself. You've accomplished so much, and you've been treated like shit by so many people."

Sighing, I pinch my lips together. "I've made lots of mistakes."

"You're thinking of Prince Dante, aren't you?"

Chuckling bitterly, I glance at Mel. "How did you know?"

"Oh, I don't know. The wistful, sad look in your eyes. The way your hand moved over your baby bump."

"That obvious, hey?" I bite my lip. "I should have been honest with him. I should have told him about the baby instead of waiting for it to come out in the media. I should have been honest about Beckett. If I'd have told him myself..."

"Look." Mel stands up, moving to sit down next to me. "Stop blaming yourself. You know what I think?"

I shake my head.

Melissa tucks her knees in and rests her chin on top of them. "I think Prince Dante's a coward. He told you he didn't care who the father was and that he'd be there for you. He told you he loved you. He told you he wanted to be by your side. Why does that suddenly change when Beckett is the father?" she scoffs. "You don't owe him anything. It's *your* choice who you tell about your pregnancy."

"It's more complicated than that."

"Is it, though?"

One thing I love about Melissa is how fiercely loyal she is. She arches her eyebrows, waiting for my response. In her mind, I'm completely in the right, and Dante is completely in the wrong.

I sigh. "I think he feels used."

"*He* feels used? Come on." Mel snorts. "He needs to get over himself."

"You don't think I should have told him about Beckett?"

"Maybe, yeah. Everything happened so fast between the two of you, though. That kind of trust takes time to build up. You had yourself and your baby to worry about. He shouldn't have kicked you out."

"He didn't. I left."

"But would you have felt welcome if you stayed?"

I grimace.

"Exactly."

"Mel, I know you're trying to be nice, but I just..."

Melissa arches her eyebrows, waiting for me to continue. I can't find the words, though, so I just shrug.

The truth is, I'm heartbroken. I feel silly for thinking that Prince Dante would be there for me, and I'm a little bit embarrassed at how quickly I fell for him.

Mel wraps me in a hug, pulling away to look in my eyes. "I have an idea."

There's a mischievous glint in her eyes, and I tilt my head. "Uh oh."

"Hear me out." She grins. "The past few months have been all over the place. You need to center yourself. You need to feel like yourself again. You are a gorgeous, strong woman. You're going to be a mother. Nothing can bring you down."

"Okay..."

Mel nods. "Photoshoot. Pregnancy announcement done *your* way. I say we go full glam, we hire the best photographer and reclaim this whole story. You need to take control of the narrative."

"You sound like Felicity."

Melissa laughs. "Maybe she's right, sometimes. Just

imagine getting fully glammed-up, looking gorgeous and glowy with your baby bump on full display. Be proud of your pregnancy. You've been hiding away for so long, and that's caused even more speculation and controversy. Why not just embrace your public image, and show everyone that you're excited to be a mother?"

I suck in a breath, already nervous at the thought of going back in front of the cameras.

"Plus," Mel adds, "nothing like a good revenge-breakup Instagram post to make a certain sulky prince jealous of how gorgeous you look."

Then, my baby kicks again, and a smile spreads across my lips. "Maybe you're right. A photoshoot could be a good idea. I like the idea of feeling beautiful again and showing people that I'm not ashamed of my pregnancy."

"Of course I'm right," Mel grins. "I'll call Felicity. I already know she'll be on board."

28

DANTE

THE DAY AFTER MARGOT LEAVES, I see photos of her getting on a plane, and photos of me looking completely crushed. Headlines scream about our breakup, about the baby, about Beckett, about Luca and Ivy's wedding.

I toss my phone away, watching the screen splinter and crack as it hits the edge of the bedside table. Wonderful. Groaning, I walk to the balcony and stare out.

Once upon a time, this view made me calm. The sight of the blue waters, gently swaying palm trees, and clear blue skies made me feel like I was at peace.

Now, it just reminds me of Margot. How she'd sit out here in the morning to have a coffee. How she looked in the morning sun. How she smiled at me from the balcony, making me feel like the most important man in the world.

She's only been in my life a short while, but I can barely remember life without her.

Theo has spent the past twenty-four hours in a panic. He's upped security on the palace and grounded all planes in an out of Argyle. The shipping ports are still operational, but under intense security. News channels talk about Prince Beckett's betrayal on a non-stop loop.

He won't find Beckett, though. I know he won't.

Our half-brother has spent the last two and a half months evading our searches—why would he be found now? He waltzed onto the private royal beach without a care in the world, knowing everything that we've been trying to keep hidden from the public.

He's always had the upper hand.

From the moment he put a baby in Margot's womb, he's had the advantage.

Roaring, I grab one of the balcony chairs and kick it as hard as I can. It skitters across the tiles and hits the balustrade with a dull thud. I pant, wanting to fling the chair off the edge or smash it to a million pieces.

With a deep breath, I resist.

Did Beckett plan this all along? Did he somehow set things up so that I would go to Farcliff, knowing I wouldn't be able to resist Margot?

Paranoia snakes through my skull, injecting venom into my thoughts. I grip the balustrade, staring out at the grounds below.

Luca and Ivy appear in the corners of my vision, walking hand-in-hand. They stop, and Luca bends down to kiss her lips. I watch as he sweeps his hands over her growing belly, resting his forehead against Ivy's.

Bitterness sticks to the back my throat.

Was I so desperate to get what they have that I fell for Margot? Was this some conspiracy that Beckett has planned from the start?

Grunting, I turn away.

I can't stand the sight of my brother's love. Even Theo and Cara together make me sick.

I wish I could go back to the time when I didn't care about finding a partner, back to a time when I was resigned to spending my days alone.

I WALLOW FOR A WEEK, while everyone else rushes to try and find Beckett.

Margot doesn't contact me, and I don't contact her. I get a new phone, but it mostly stays untouched on my bedside table.

Then, a couple of photos start appearing everywhere I look. Every internet news website, every newspaper, every celebrity blog.

Margot stares back with a protective hand over her little, twenty-two week baby bump and a soft smile on her lips.

She looks fucking gorgeous, and my heart breaks all over again. Whenever I look at a screen, her beautiful face stares back at me.

She's not wearing hair extensions, and her bump is exposed for the camera. She looks completely unapologetic, and I can't help but feel like she did it for my benefit.

I don't need you, Margot screams through the photos. *I'll be fine without you.*

For the first time since she left, my anger fades. The roaring of rage quiets down in my ears, and another voice speaks up.

Maybe I was wrong.

It's a bitter pill to swallow, and one I'm not quite ready to accept—but everywhere I look, there she is. Beautiful. Strong. Proud.

Alone.

Then, the voice gets louder: I should be by her side. She shouldn't need to be facing this on her own.

Didn't I tell her that I didn't care who the father was?

I turn away from the photos, shutting all my screens down and forcing myself to stay off the internet. I can't look at her. I can't face the shame of abandoning a pregnant woman just because of my own sick vanity.

So, I cling on to the idea that Beckett masterminded it all. Margot must have been in on it. She must have plotted with Beckett to bring down Luca and her sister. She's vindictive and jealous, and she tricked me into loving her.

I have to believe those horrible thoughts, because the alternative is admitting that I was wrong. The alternative means that Margot is on her own in Farcliff, facing the birth of a child fathered by an attempted murderer. The alternative means I'm the lowest, most cowardly excuse of a man to ever wander this earth.

I let my anger grow louder again. I let bitterness rise up in my throat, and the sound of my own pride drowns out any other thoughts.

29

IVY

LUCA IS TENSE. Margot is gone. Dante is angry. King Theo is worried, and the entire Kingdom is in turmoil.

And me?

I waddle around and try to keep it together. I talk to my twins day and night, singing softly to them to try to soothe my own worries. I make my way to the kitchens and bake late into the night, just to distract myself from the troubles that surround me.

About a week after Margot leaves, I'm in the kitchen making my signature cinnamon buns. When I start dicing the apples for the filling, the knife slips and slices across my finger. Wincing, I bring the finger up to my mouth as blood beads over the cut.

"Damn it," I whisper to myself, walking to the sink. My hands are trembling and my breath is shaky.

This isn't what I expected when I got married to Luca. Somehow, I thought that getting married would make things easier, but everything just seems to be falling apart more and more.

Letting water run over my cut, I drop my shoulders and let out a sigh.

Everything is upside down. Luca doesn't want me to go back to Farcliff until Beckett is found, but I feel like I should be with my sister and my bakery. The twins assure me that *Spoonful of Sugar* is in good hands, but that bakery was my first baby.

Glancing down at my growing belly, I let out a sigh.

I just hope Beckett is found before my babies are born. In my heart of hearts, I know Luca is right about staying here. I need him by my side, and he needs to be in Argyle for his family.

Pulling out my phone, I dial Margot's number.

"Hey, Poison," she answers, using Luca's nickname for me.

I smile. "Hey, Margie."

My sister chuckles. "You know, it used to really bother me when you used my real name, but now I kind of like it."

"It reminds me of Mom." Tears start to sting my eyes. I turn the water off and wrap my finger in a clean towel, leaning on the kitchen counter.

"Me too," Margot answers. Her voice sounds small, and I hear her sigh over the phone. "A lot of things remind me of her these days."

"Are you okay? I wish you were still here."

"I'm not welcome in Argyle, Ivy."

"Of course you are. You're my sister. Dante would come around... He's just a man who had his pride hurt."

"I'm sorry I didn't tell you about Beckett."

"You don't have to tell me anything," I answer.

"It was only one time," Margot says. She groans, and I hear some rustling as if she's moving to sit or lie down. "The night that I OD'd, I felt so lonely, and he was there..."

"And Dante thinks you planned the whole thing?"

"Yeah. He said he thought I was using him, that I just jumped from one brother to the next."

"Ugh," I groan. "Men."

Margot laughs. "You've changed, Ivy. You're talking like a grizzled divorcée, not someone who met the love of her life and married him in a tropical palace."

"Well, yeah," I laugh. "But still." I take a deep breath. "I saw your pictures online. You look great."

"That was Mel's idea," Margot replies. "She said it would help me take control of my image and my pregnancy again."

"And did it?"

My sister is quiet for a moment. I can sense that she's holding something back from me, but I don't know what. As we listen to each other breathing on either end of the phone, my chest squeezes.

We've been so close for so many years, but still so distant from each other. I didn't know she was lonely or unhappy. I just thought she was living the dream.

Peeling the edge of the dishtowel off my finger, I see that the bleeding has stopped. Margot still hasn't said anything.

"Hey, Margie," I start softly.

"Yeah?"

"You know I love you, right? No matter what? And I don't think for a second that you were using Dante. I could see you were happier than you've been in years when you were with him."

Margot lets a sob out so quietly that I hardly hear it. She inhales, and I imagine her nodding. "I love you too, Ivy. I got to go. I'll talk to you later."

"Okay," I answer, my heart sinking when I hear the phone click.

Something is definitely wrong. My sister has always kept up the appearance of being happy, even when she wasn't—but something has changed. Her brightness has dimmed.

Glancing at my half-finished cinnamon buns, I grab the dough and pop it in the refrigerator. Scooping the diced apples into a container, I put them beside the dough and wipe down the counter before heading up to my bedroom to sleep.

THAT NIGHT, I toss and turn so much that in the middle of the night, Luca asks me if everything's okay. I mumble something in response and force myself to sit still, finally falling asleep for an hour or two just as the sun comes up.

Bleary-eyed, I wake up to the smell of coffee. Luca sits on the bed beside me, pushing a strand of hair off my forehead.

"Morning, gorgeous."

"Hey," I smile.

"I want to show you something today."

"Right now?"

Luca nods. He smiles, but it's not his usual broad, open smile. His eyes look tired, and he squeezes my hand before standing up.

I get dressed quickly, rubbing the sleep out of my eyes and gulping down the scorching-hot coffee. I don't even have the energy to think about not drinking it. The doctor said a coffee once in a while was okay. Luca must have known I'd need it.

My husband slips his hand into mine and leads me out to the palace grounds.

"Where are you taking me?"

"You'll see. I haven't been here in years, but somehow it feels like the right time to go there."

Luca leads me to a small dirt path at the back of the

castle. As it winds up through the palace grounds, my pulse quickens.

Luca is quiet, his steps hurried. I glance up to see Luca's brows drawn together and his lips pinched in a thin line.

I think I know where we're going.

When the path starts winding upward, it feels like one of the first days we met, when we jumped off the cliff into Farcliff Lake together. When everything was exciting and new, and when I first started falling in love with him.

The path narrows, and I let Luca take the lead. I can see the tension rippling across his shoulders. I wish I could run my fingers over their breadth, soothing his troubled spirit.

Instead, I just follow.

Luca speeds up, racing through the trees to scramble up the final rocky outcropping to the flat patch of land on top of the cliff. He turns to help me up over the last rocks, putting a protective arm across my back to help me up the rest of the way.

When I get to the top, a warm breeze whips around me. I take a deep breath, inhaling the salty, fresh ocean air, closing my eyes and letting the moment settle in.

"This is it," Luca says simply. "It's where everything started. The top of the cliff, where I jumped off and landed in the shallow water. The spot on this earth where I broke my back, shattering my chances with Cara and changing the course of my life forever. The series of events that led me to you."

Luca turns to stare into my eyes, wrapping his arms around my waist and leaning his head against mine.

I watch him swallow, turning to look out at the turquoise waters. "I haven't been back here since the accident," he continues. "But it felt like it was time."

"How come?"

"I don't know. Time for me to move on, maybe, once and for all." A soft smile stretches his lips, and he turns his eyes back to me. "My accident defined me for so long, but I don't want that anymore. I thought I'd never come back here. I thought I'd never face my past as I'm facing it now. Over the past few months, I've developed a strength that I never knew I had. It's because of you—I know it is. You've shown me what it means to be brave, tenacious, and strong."

My Prince drops his lips to mine, and my heart is so filled with love and joy that I feel like I'm going to burst. Our twins start fluttering in my stomach so hard that even Luca feels them against him. We laugh, looking down at our children as they kick with us.

"Love you," Luca says, kissing my forehead.

Before I can answer, a noise interrupts us. Someone sneezes from behind the tree line.

"Well, well, well," a voice calls out. "I never thought I'd see you up here again."

I turn to see Luca's half-brother Beckett walk out from behind a tree. His beard has grown, and he looks like he hasn't showered in days. He sneezes again, swearing softly as he rubs his nose. Luca stiffens, moving in front of me to block me from his brother's gaze.

"Have you been hiding out here this whole time?" The tension is back in Luca's shoulders.

Beckett grunts, staring at the two of us with beady, black eyes. He peers over Luca's shoulder at me, and a chill courses down my spine.

"What do you want, Beckett?" Luca's voice is gruff. Angry. Menacing.

"I want you to finish what we started five years ago." He jerks his head to the cliff. "You should have died that day."

Something in the way his brother's lips curl makes my blood turn to ice. My heart thumps.

"What are you talking about?" I croak from behind Luca's back.

"I said, you should have died that day. Everyone knows it. But no, you had to live, because everything you do is so fucking *perfect*. You couldn't just be a mortal, for once." Beckett scoffs, staring at the two of us with a razor-sharp gaze.

I can feel his hatred slicing through me. I wince.

Beckett takes a step toward us. "You even brought your pregnant wife up here, just to rub my nose in how much better your life turned out than mine."

"I didn't even know you were up here, Beckett." Luca moves slowly, pulling his cell phone out of his pants pocket. He hands it to me behind his back, and I know he wants me to call for help.

Beckett looks like he's in his own world. He combs his fingers through his beard, staring at Luca with bone-chilling hatred. "Do you remember that day, brother? Because I do. I knew that water was too shallow, but I convinced you to jump, anyway." Beckett scoffs, shaking his head. "I thought it would bring Cara and me closer together. I thought I could take your place. All I did was create the fucking demi-god that you've become."

The two of them face off in front of each other. My pulse feels thick and sluggish in my veins as my mind whirls around me, and my hands just won't cooperate. I can't get Luca's phone unlocked, and then I notice there's no signal. My eyes dart back up to the two brothers. Luca's still standing protectively between the two of us, and Beckett is starting to circle to the left, pinning us next to the cliff's edge.

"You didn't convince me to jump," Luca says slowly. "I'd wanted to do it for weeks."

"And who planted the idea in the first place?" Beckett scoffs. "You've always been easy to lead."

"No." The Prince shakes his head. "No, you're lying."

Beckett barks out a laugh, rolling his eyes. "It was pointless, anyway. Cara didn't want me. She upgraded to Theo. Why be the bastard boy's wife when you can be a queen?"

Slowly, second by second, moment by moment, Beckett's words are starting to sink in.

He was in love with Cara.

He tried to kill Luca...multiple times. He tried to get him to break his back, and then came back five years later to finish the job with pills. This wasn't a new twist of events in the past couple of months. It's been going on for *years.*

Understanding must register on my face, because Beckett starts to laugh. It doesn't sound like his carefree, musical laugh. It's unhinged. It's evil.

"And your fucking sister had to live, too. Stupid bitch," Beckett spits at me, his mouth twisting into an ugly snarl. "I thought I gave her enough to kill an elephant, but she survived."

My heart stops. The overdose.

It wasn't Margot's fault at all. I'd always been confused about the drugs. I thought I'd been blind, and that she was still hiding something from me.

It was all Beckett.

Before I can react, he lunges for us. Luca is quicker. He grabs Beckett across the middle and tackles him to the ground. I scream, the sound ripping my vocal cords raw. They roll over, and Luca's head lands an inch away from the edge. Beckett's fingers wrap around his neck.

"This'll end today," he growls, inching Luca closer to the edge. "You'll lose everything, including your new wife."

I scream. I move closer, but Luca waves me away, gasping.

I don't know what to do. I'm useless.

Luca's phone isn't working. I don't have mine. I can't run and get help while my husband is being strangled on the edge of a cliff. I can't jump in and help, because they're both stronger than me and I have two babies to worry about.

So, I just stand there, helpless.

With Beckett's hand on Luca's windpipe, I can see Luca's strength sapping away. His movements are getting heavier, and his eyes bulge unnaturally. I scream again, taking a step closer to them. Luca struggles against his half-brother, grunting.

Luca told me that the first time Beckett attacked him, he couldn't hit his brother. It felt wrong.

Now, though, I can see in Luca's eyes that he knows this is life or death. Beckett isn't his brother anymore. I scream again, urging him to fight back. With the last bit of his power, Luca lands a punch to the kidneys. Beckett winces, releasing his grasp on Luca's neck long enough for Luca to flip him over.

Beckett claws at Luca's face, tearing jagged, bloody lines down his cheek. I scream, scrambling toward them and grabbing Beckett around the neck.

"Ivy, no!" Luca screams just as Beckett flings me back. I fall back, landing on jagged rocks. I cradle my stomach, just wanting to protect my children. A scream slips through my lips just as Luca punches his brother in the jaw. Beckett knees him in the groin and pain shatters visibly across Luca's face. Using Luca's moment of weakness, Beckett rolls them over again.

I groan, peeling myself off the rocks and crawling away. Tears are streaming down my face.

"Run, Ivy! Get help." Luca struggles with Beckett, but I can't leave.

I just can't.

The wind whips around us. I can smell the sour sweat on Beckett's body, the salty air, the fresh breeze through the trees.

I don't want Luca to die.

Scanning the rocks, I find one that fits into my hand. Rasping, I pick it up and turn toward the men. I'm going to end this right now. No one hurts my Luca.

No one.

As I stalk toward the two men, I see something change in Luca. He can see me approaching. With his last ounce of strength, Luca lands a punch to Beckett's temple. A wheeze escapes the man's lips, and he slumps to the side. Beckett's body goes limp, and he falls toward the edge of the cliff.

Too close. His legs slip over the edge, followed by his hips, his chest.

Screaming, Luca reaches for him. He manages to grab onto his brother's arm with one hand and Beckett's belt with the other.

Luca roars, and I don't know if it's panic or pain. Blood is pouring from a cut above his eye. His face is scratched, his knuckles bloody. I drop the rock, scrambling toward them. I ignore my own pain as it burns through my body. My back is in agony. Every nerve ending is burning, twisting, piercing through me.

Grunting, Luca tries to haul his brother to safety. He stumbles, and Beckett's limp body starts to slip from his grasp. I pant, dropping to my knees to grab Beckett's arm.

Luca closes my eyes for just a moment to try to clear his head.

I see him hesitate, and I know what he's feeling. I know, because we're one person split into two bodies. Luca is my soulmate, the love of my life, the father of my children.

I know the look on his face.

There's too much pain in his body. Too much suffering in his heart. If he just loosens his grip, Beckett will fall, and it'll all be over.

"Luca," I say softly. "On three."

Luca huffs, opening his eyes again and nodding.

"One," I say, sending love and support into Luca's soul.

"Two." Strength pulses from me to him, and the knowledge that the guilt of Beckett's death would kill him eventually. We have to save Beckett—even though they're only half related, even though he tried to kill Luca, even though he poisoned Margot, even though he did it all out of sick jealousy—we can't let him fall.

"Three."

Luca lets out a wordless scream, pulling Beckett up over the edge. Beckett's limp body lands on top of my husband's, and I help to roll Beckett over onto his back. His head lolls to the side, his tongue hanging out.

Panting, Luca feels for a pulse. He nods.

Beckett's still alive.

I let out a breath, closing my eyes for just a moment. Then, I pick myself up off the ground. Luca stands up with me, wrapping his arms around me as tears start to fall from his eyes.

"I'm sorry," he says, over and over again. "I'm so sorry, Ivy."

"Shh," I say. I don't have the energy to say anything else. I just nod, kissing Luca's tears away and nodding to Beckett. "Let's deal with him."

Beckett is too heavy to drag or carry back down to the palace, so we scrounge around for something to tie him with.

The only thing we have is our shoelaces. I take them off my shoes and hand them to Luca, who does his best to bind his brother's hands and feet. I pray that he'll still be here when the guards come back.

Then, the two of us stumble back as fast as our screaming bodies will let us. I wave Luca ahead. "I need to go slow," I say, putting a hand to my stomach. "You go get help."

"You've got to be crazy if you think I'm leaving you, Ivy," Luca says, dropping back to stay by my side. "We do this together."

My lower lip trembles as a wave of emotion crashes into me.

Luca slides his hand over my shoulders and holds me close. "It's over now, Ivy, my love. It's all over."

I nod, not trusting my voice. Tears stream down my face as his words sink in.

It's all over.

Now, we can live. Now, we can be free. Now, we can move forward.

30

MARGOT

I'VE BEEN SPENDING MORE time at *Spoonful of Sugar* since I got back to Farcliff. Giselle and Georgina have been running the place since Ivy's been gone, and it's nice to have some familiar faces around. In a way, being at the bakery feels more like home than the big mansion where I sleep.

One evening, Ivy calls me, breathless, and tells me they caught Beckett. She tells them he confessed to injecting me with heroin laced with fentanyl, causing my overdose. A tear drops from my eye, and all I do is cradle my stomach.

A part of me expects to get a call from Dante.

I don't, though. Why would he call?

Catching Beckett doesn't change anything. He's the father of my child. I withheld that information from Dante. Just because Beckett is behind bars doesn't mean that Dante's opinion of me has changed.

I mostly work in the back of the bakery, doing odd jobs and keeping myself busy. Even though Felicity and Melissa want me to get back into the public eye, I've been enjoying spending time with people like the twins and their brothers.

They don't treat me like a celebrity. I'm not Margot

LeBlanc to the seven of them, I'm just Ivy's sister. Plus, my baby kicks happily anytime I'm at the bakery, and who am I to resist that kind of endorsement? Whether it's the smells of delicious baking, or the laughter and camaraderie of the twins and other workers, I'm not sure.

Either way, it's where I want to be.

Irving, the twins' oldest brother, usually elicits lots of kicks from the baby. His big, booming voice and constant supply of milkshakes keeps both me and my child happy.

"Any plans for the holidays, Margot?" Irving asks, hauling a huge bag of flour over his shoulder. "Christmas is only two weeks away."

"Just going to take it easy," I respond, trying to keep the grimace off my face.

Last year, the holidays were full of celebrity-studded parties, drinking, drugs, and time spent with Ivy. This year, my sister is in Argyle and I have no desire to go out.

"Well, you have to come to our place," Giselle says, poking her pink head of hair through the door. "Georgie and I are making a turkey."

"With my help," Irving grins. "Don't know that I'd trust the two of you with a bird that big."

Giselle laughs, waving him away. "Fine. We'll make the pies, then."

My heart warms and I nod. "That would be great, actually."

"What's Ivy going to do?"

"I think she's staying in Argyle."

Giselle smiles sadly. "I miss her, but I get that she wants to be with her new hubby."

"That's exactly how I feel."

Giselle walks over to me and wraps her arms around my shoulders. "Well, you can be our replacement Ivy."

I laugh. "Never thought I'd hear those words."

"Got to knock you down a peg or two," Irving grins. "Too much celebrity and fame aren't good for a person."

"You're probably right."

My baby moves, and I put a hand to my stomach. Taking a deep breath, a sense of calm washes over me. A few months ago, I would have been unhappy and panicking about the holidays.

It's harder to face your demons without chemical numbness, but it feels good. Now, I feel all my emotions fully. I still feel sad about Dante's reaction. A part of me wishes that he'd stepped up and accepted my child and me like he said he would.

I trusted him when he said he loved me. I believed him when he said he wanted this child like his own.

I should have known the truth.

It's too hard to take on someone else's burden like that. There are too many forces working against us, and too many reasons for him to turn away. Better for me to know now, than to start to rely on his love and support only to be crushed after the baby is born.

He was quick to turn his back on me when he found out about the baby's father. Imagine how he would have reacted if he found out about my disease!

No, I'm better off on my own. That way, I can rely on my own strength. I know I won't let myself down.

At least, that's what I tell myself.

My heart is always in agony when I think of the betrayal on Dante's face when he found out about Beckett. Nights are lonely, and I miss his touch, his kiss, his sex.

But I refuse to let myself wallow.

I'm stronger now. I've changed. I'm no longer the sick, weak girl who was constantly looking for approval from others. Although I miss Ivy, I don't begrudge her spending time with her new family. I don't chase photo opportunities with the paparazzi, or crave the validation of the masses.

I'm lonely, but I'm not alone.

I keep my hands busy at the bakery, and my mind busy with my baby.

Still, I see Dante everywhere. I see him in the walk-in fridge, where he pushed me up against the wall and made me come for the first time. I see him at the house, near the pool, in my bed. The wind carries his smell, and I imagine his face on a thousand different strangers in the street.

He's not here, though, and I'm better off alone.

So, the week before Christmas, when Ivy walks through the front door, I almost drop the tray of cookies that I'm carrying to the display case.

Georgie squeals, jumping over the counter and wrapping her arms around Ivy. Prince Luca stiffens beside her, putting a protective hand over Ivy's back.

Once the twins release my sister from their grasp, Ivy moves toward me. She gives me a big hug, glancing down at my belly.

"Don't we look like a pair of whales."

"Speak for yourself, Ivy," I shoot back, laughing as I wrap my arms around her again. "What are you doing here? I thought you were spending the holidays in Argyle."

"She insisted," Luca interjects, putting an arm around my shoulders. "Couldn't spend Christmas without you. Maybe the bakery, too. Argyle Palace is overrun with cinnamon buns. Can't find enough people to eat them all."

Ivy laughs, elbowing him in the ribs. Her eyes shine as she looks around the bakery, already reaching for an apron.

"Definitely came back for the bakery," I grin, glancing at Luca.

THAT NIGHT, it actually feels good to go back home with Ivy. It's not a big, empty house anymore. It's home. As Ivy and I lay back on the couches in the living room and she fills me in on everything that's happened in Argyle, my mind drifts to Dante.

A pulsing pain passes through my chest, just like it always does when I think of him. I blame myself for our breakup, but I still resent him for not loving me like he promised he would.

After the heartbreak of leaving him behind, and the excruciating pain of his silence, I learned one thing: I should have told him about everything. I should have been honest with him from the start about the baby, about Beckett, even about my disease.

Starting a relationship with him under false pretenses was wrong, and that's why it fell apart. Of course, he could have acted more graciously. Of course, he could have been kinder. Of course, he could have loved me anyway.

But I'm the one that lied by omission. I'm the one that was too much of a coward to say anything.

If there's one thing I've learned over the past few months, it's that I need to be more honest with everyone—including myself. I don't want my child to grow up with a mother who's afraid to face her demons, or who can't say how she feels. I don't want to hide my illness from my sister and my child. I don't want to die quietly, like Mama did. I want to *live*. Even if it isn't the longest life, I want to live it to its fullest.

I'm sick of being afraid. I'm sick of being small.

"Dante's been struggling." Ivy glances at me, and the sound of the Prince's name makes my ears perk up.

I clear my throat. "What do you mean?"

"He's been mopey and weird since you left. Luca says that's how he was when he was younger. He'll disappear for days at a time and barely talks to anyone."

"Oh." I'm not quite sure what to do with that information. By the way Ivy is staring at me, I can tell my response isn't enough for her.

Silence hangs between us. I stare at the ceiling, and for the first time, I realize that the only way for me to live my life is if I'm completely open. Honest. Free.

"I have Huntington's."

The revelation just falls out of my mouth. I hadn't even intended on telling her tonight. I knew I wanted to tell her, but I didn't know it would happen like this.

Ivy stares at me blankly. "What?"

I turn my head to meet her gaze, swallowing thickly. I nod. "Yeah."

"Since when?"

"Well, I'm guessing since I was born. It is genetic, after all."

"Don't be a dick," Ivy grunts. "When did you find out? We both got tested. It was negative!"

I shake my head. "*Yours* was negative."

"You've been positive for six months? Since before..."

"I found out the day I slept with Beckett. The day he made me overdose." I sigh, shaking my head. "Worst day of my life."

Ivy's bottom lip trembles and her eyes fill with tears. "Why didn't you tell me?" Her voice is barely above a whisper.

I heave myself off the sofa, moving to sit beside her. Wrapping my arms around my sister, I hold her close.

"I was scared," I answer simply. "Then, I found out about the baby..."

"Is the baby okay?"

I give her a tight smile. "I decided not to get the test."

"But..."

"I know. I just couldn't face the decision I'd have to make if it was positive." I smile sadly. "I never said I was brave. I just said I have Huntington's."

Ivy nods, wiping a tear from her cheek. I smile at my sister, squeezing her closer. She cries into my chest, and I pat her head and rock her back and forth.

I don't feel sad.

I feel free.

I said the words out loud, and I didn't get hit by a bolt of lightning. Nothing bad happened, apart from Ivy's tears.

The truth is out there now.

I have Huntington's disease. Over the next fifteen or twenty years, I'll develop twitches and jerks. I'll lose control over my movements. I might have trouble walking, talking, swallowing. My personality will likely change and I'll have trouble reasoning.

I'll die young.

All those things are true, and I've said it out loud. Now, Ivy knows the truth, too.

I'm no longer afraid.

31

DANTE

I THOUGHT things would get easier when Beckett was found.

They haven't.

Theo looks like he's aged ten years in the last ten days. I've isolated myself again, hiding from cameras and people like I used to.

All the while, I think of Margot.

After Ivy and Luca leave for Farcliff, I feel Margot's absence even more.

Still, I can't get over her betrayal. The fact that she jumped from Luca, to Beckett, and finally to me is just too much to cope with. I told her I *loved* her. She thought she got what she wanted out of me. I was just the poor idiot that would take care of her unwanted kid.

That's what I tell myself, anyway.

Late at night, though, when I stare up at the ceiling and I miss the sound of her breathing, I wonder if it might just be my pride talking.

The day after Luca and Ivy leave, I make my way to the Argyle prison. Beckett is being held in a special holding cell, kept under close custody.

Taking a deep breath as the guards lead me to his cell, I clench my fists and grind my teeth. I'm not sure I'm ready for this.

My brother looks up from his cot when the guard opens the door. A cruel smile stretches his lips.

"Dante," he croons, spreading his arms wide. "So nice of you to come visit, brother."

"Good to see you've finally showered. You were looking pretty awful last time we spoke."

Beckett bares his teeth.

The guard closes the door behind me. I pull a chair over and take a seat, clasping my hands in front of me and staring at my brother.

"What brings you to my neck of the woods?" Beckett asks, leaning back against the concrete wall as if any of this is normal.

"Why did you do it?"

"Do what?"

"Try to hurt Luca? All he's ever done is try to keep our family together after Mother betrayed Father."

Beckett scoffs. "Yeah, right. Luca, the perfect son. The cripple turned miracle. Give me a fucking break."

"What's your problem, Beckett?"

"My problem?" Beckett swings his eyes to me. His gaze is dark and unreadable. "My problem is that my whole life, I've never been good enough for this fucking family. Mother treated me like I was a lost puppy that she saved, and the King did nothing but belittle me and make me feel like an outsider."

Beckett's chest heaves. I gulp, not knowing how to answer. The last thing I want to do is agitate him.

He scoffs, straightening his prison uniform and combing his fingers through his hair. "Luca was the worst of them all.

Daddy's favorite. The athlete. The jokester. How any of you guys stand him is beyond me. After Mother ran off, he took up the role of my chief torturer."

"Luca? He loved you. He always thought of you as a brother."

"Is that what you call it? Parading Cara in front of me when he knew I was in love with her? Making fun of me every time I tagged along, making me feel like I was never welcome? Yeah, right. He deserved to jump off that cliff and break his back."

Clasping my hands together, I try my best to hide the swell of anger in my heart. No one deserves to break their back.

I don't even know why I'm here. I have nothing to say to Beckett, but I thought maybe I could get some answers from him. Maybe, talking to him, I could understand what happened between him and Margot.

Now that I see him, though, I know I won't get anything from him. I push myself off the chair and move toward the cell door.

"You're just as bad as he is," Beckett says to my back.

I turn to face him, grinding my teeth. "Yeah? How do you figure?"

"You never saw me as a brother."

"I always saw you as a brother, Beckett. Just as much as Theo or Luca. You were the one who stood in my corner when I wanted to stay out of the public eye. You always defended my right to privacy to Mother and Father. I loved you."

"Past tense? You don't love me anymore?"

We stare at each other, and I shake my head. "I can't forgive what you did to Luca."

Beckett arches an eyebrow. "Only Luca? What about Margot?"

My brother laughs when he sees the tension ratchet up in my body. I clench my fists at the sound of her name, betraying why I'm really here.

"Well, you can have her," Beckett spits, laying down in bed and turning his back to me. "She was a mediocre fuck, anyway. Once was enough for me. Turns out, Luca didn't even care about her, and she looked just as bored as I was. She didn't even have the decency to die like she was supposed to." He pulls his thin blanket up to his chin without another word, and I know the conversation is over.

I rap my knuckles on the door and the guard opens it a second later. As I walk back down the prison hallways, my mind whirls, and I realize I was wrong.

Margot didn't have a master plan. She wasn't trying to use me. Beckett was using *her*.

He left her, pregnant and alone, confused as to how she ended up overdosing while he moved on to other ways to hurt Luca.

And me?

I'm no better. I broke down her defenses one by one and convinced her to trust me. I wormed my way into her heart and then I left her behind.

I'm just the same as Beckett, if not worse.

WHEN I GET BACK to Argyle Palace, I feel empty. Alone.

I feel like an ass.

Throwing a few things into a bag, I ask for the jet to be prepared. Then, I find Theo and Cara and say a quick good-bye. Theo nods to me, his face somber. I don't have to tell him why I'm leaving—he understands. Ever since he started dating Cara, he's understood matters of the heart better than any of the rest of us.

None of us—not Theo, Luca, Beckett, or me—ever do things the easy way, apparently.

So, I sling my bag over my shoulder and stride to the waiting royal vehicle.

I'm going to Farcliff.

The plane takes off, and my heart starts pumping harder. My knee bounces up and down, and I chew on my nails as we make the three-hour flight up to Farcliff. I wave the flight attendants away and stare out the window at the setting sun, taking deep, cleansing breaths.

When we land, it's far colder than I ever expected. It's the week before Christmas, and the air in Farcliff is full of holiday fervor.

I jump in a car and give Margot's address, tugging at my collar as I start to sweat.

Suddenly, it seems too impulsive to be here. I should have called Margot. I should have tried to text her or warn her in some way that I was coming.

But what could I say? I need to see her face when I tell her that I was wrong. I need to hold her in my arms and smell her skin before dropping to my knees and asking for her forgiveness.

I don't know how I'll prove to her that I'm worthy of her love, but I'll find a way.

Hope blooms in my heart as my love for Margot flares. All the emotion that I've kept at bay comes back with a vengeance, and all I can think about is how much I care about her.

I was a fool to push her away. An idiot to doubt her. An ass to let her leave.

That changes right now.

The car pulls through the gates, and a few stray photographers snap pictures of my car. I wince, and then brace myself against the cameras. They can't see me through the tinted windows.

In any case, this is what I need to get used to. If I'm going to prove myself to Margot, I need to show her that I can handle the public scrutiny and her life as a celebrity. I can live my life in the open and I can change my ways, because I love her.

I love her more than anything in the world, and I need her in my life.

Those words play on repeat in my mind as the driver opens my door for me. I nod to him, my eyes trained on the front door.

My hands tremble as I raise a fist to knock. With a deep breath, I rap on the door, and I wait.

32

MARGOT

IVY IS STILL CRYING in my arms when a knock comes on the door. We both stiffen, my sister wiping the tears from her eyes and glancing over her shoulder.

"Who is it?"

"I'm not sure," I answer.

"Tell them to go away."

I laugh. "I will."

Giving her shoulders one last squeeze, I extricate myself from my sister's hold. Brushing my hands over my thighs, I try to straighten up my crumpled clothing as I walk to the front door.

Maybe Luca ordered pizza, or some reporter got through security somehow. Maybe Felicity came by with some last-minute plans for my upcoming week of public appearances.

I run through every single possibility, except one.

Shock registers on my face as I swing the door open. Dante stands on the porch, arms hanging at his sides, face betraying no tension. He inhales sharply when he sees me, but otherwise says nothing.

He looks gorgeous.

Rugged, haunted, and exactly like the man who has been plaguing my dreams. His eyes stare into me, begging me to let him in. I fight it with every ounce of my strength. I brace myself against the assault that his gaze wages on me, bolstering the defenses around my heart.

He kicked me out. He turned his back on me. He left me out in the cold.

Now, without a word, I'm ready to let him back in?

My heart stutters as a soft breeze carries his scent toward me. I close my eyes for a brief moment.

I thought I was strong. I thought I was free, and ready to live honestly. I thought I wanted to proclaim my illness from the rooftops with pride, ready to conquer whatever the world had to throw at me. I thought I could raise my baby on my own and stand on my own two feet.

The Prince makes me crumble with one look. He hasn't even said a single word, and I'm ready to open myself back up to him.

"Dante," I finally manage to croak, clearing my throat and patting my hair.

"Margot." His voice is husky, barely a breath.

"I... What are you doing here?"

"I came to see you."

"Dante!" Ivy says behind my shoulder. "I thought you were still in Argyle."

"I flew back," he says, moving his gaze from me to my sister and back to me again.

I know he's waiting for me to open the door wider. He's expecting me to let him in.

But how could I?

The man who broke my heart is standing there like nothing at all is wrong. His face is open, and although his eyes betray a bit of pain, it's nothing compared with the suffering in my heart.

I gulp, frozen in place. My feet grow roots and I can't move from my spot on the floor.

"Can I...come in?" Dante arches his eyebrows.

I nod, pulling the door wider, but instead of waiting around to see what he has to say, I mumble something incoherent and escape up the stairs.

Only when I'm safe in my room do I let a breath out and sink onto the floor. Dropping my head in my hands, I finally let a sob rack through my body. All the tears I've held inside come rushing out and I curse my miserable life. I cry for my mother, for my childhood, for all my failed relationships and the weaknesses that have plagued my entire existence.

If I were stronger, I wouldn't have fallen prey to celebrity and all its curses. If I were stronger, I would have been honest with Dante about the baby.

If I were stronger, I wouldn't be so fucking terrified of dying.

Huddling on the floor, I cry into the carpet and clutch my growing belly.

"Margie?" Ivy knocks softly on my door, barely whispering my name.

"What?"

She tries to open the door, but my body blocks her from opening it more than an inch or two.

"Margot," she says softly, "will you let me in?"

Crawling to my hands and knees, I scoot out of the way. I lean against the wall and watch as my sister walks in and slides down the wall beside me. We sit there, knees up, pregnant stomachs protruding, staring straight ahead.

"He's here for you," Ivy finally whispers.

"So?"

"So, don't you want to talk to him?"

"Not particularly, no." I try to laugh, but it turns into an awful snort. Wiping my cheeks with my palms, I take a deep, shaking breath. "I don't have anything to say to him."

"You still love him."

"I don't see how that's relevant."

Ivy snorts, shaking her head. "Don't you?"

"Look, Ivy, we don't all get happily ever afters like you, okay? Maybe this is exactly what I deserve. I've lived my life hiding from everything bad, taking the easy way out every time I could. Even with Dante, I hid my pregnancy and the fact that Beckett is the father from him, and it blew up in my face." My breath shakes, and I squeeze my eyes shut. "Today, I decided I wasn't going to live like that anymore. I told you about my disease because I wanted to be honest and strong and open."

"And hiding from the man who loves you is being honest, and strong, and open?"

"No," I laugh bitterly. My eyes are still leaking tears, and I wipe them away with frustration. I don't want to cry! I don't want to hide!

But what else can I do?

"If I go down there, I'll end up kissing him. He'll say he's sorry and I'll say I'm sorry and that will be the end of it, but that's not good enough."

Ivy's silent for a while, and she finally takes a deep breath. "Why not?"

I stare at my sister. "What do you mean?"

"Why isn't sorry good enough?"

"Because it's not, Ivy. There's too much between us. We've only known each other a couple of months, and there are too many things stacked up against our relationship. If we break so easily, so early on, what hope do we have in the long run? I don't want to prolong my pain. I just want to stand on my own two feet and give my child the stability it deserves."

Ivy sighs, leaning her head against my shoulder. "That makes sense, I guess. It just seems like a shame to throw it all away."

"I'm not throwing anything away," I say, mostly to convince myself. "I don't have anything to throw away to begin with. I'm trying to be a better person. What kind of person would I be if I just ran back into the arms of someone who basically threw me out when he found out who the father of my kid is?"

"You want me to ask him to leave?"

"Yes. No. Maybe."

Ivy laughs, and I chuckle, shaking my head.

"I'll go talk to him," I say, pushing myself up to my feet. I help my sister up, and we both take a moment to catch our breath.

"I don't think sitting on the floor will be a part of my life for the next few months," Ivy says, grinning at me. "That was far too difficult."

"Agreed."

Ivy wraps her arm around my waist and leans her cheek against my shoulder. "It'll work out," she says. "It always does."

Forcing a smile, I just nod. I don't want to tell her that things always seem to work out for her. Me, on the other hand? Things only seem to fall apart.

With a sigh, I open my bedroom door and head downstairs to find Dante.

33

DANTE

I DON'T KNOW what kind of welcome I was expecting, but it wasn't that. When Ivy disappears to go chase after Margot, I wander to the back of the house and stare out the sliding glass doors to the backyard beyond.

A heavy hand lands on my shoulder, and Luca wraps me in a quick hug.

"Didn't think I'd see you here."

"It had to be done," I say, forcing a smile.

Inside, I'm barely holding it together. The hope that flared inside me is slowly dying, taking my heart with it. If Margot doesn't talk to me soon, I might suffocate from my own stress.

Luca lets out a deep sigh, walking away and leaving me to stare out the window by myself.

I'm not sure how much time goes by, but after a while, someone clears their throat behind me. I turn to see Margot standing at the entrance to the living room, looking as beautiful and as radiant as ever.

How did I ever turn my back on her? How did I ever make her feel like she wasn't the one for me?

There's no one else. Never has been, never will be.

I promised that I'd be by her side, and then I turned my back on her.

For what?

For my own pride. My own twisted past. My own prejudices.

"Margot," I say.

"Hi." She pads into the living room and sits down on a couch with a sigh, cupping her hands under her stomach.

I desperately want to run my hands over her bump. I want to lay a kiss on it, and talk to the baby inside. Because as stupid as I've been, I know in my heart that I want that baby to be mine. Even if it carries Beckett's DNA, it's always been my baby. *Our* baby.

Instead of sitting beside her, though, I take a seat on the armchair to her left. I lean my elbows on my knees, tenting my fingers and staring at the carpet.

"So, you're here," she starts. I can feel her eyes on me, but I'm too scared to look at her. If I meet her eye and I see nothing but pain, I know it'll be over.

"I'm here," I finally respond. With a sigh, I force myself to meet her gaze.

"Why?"

My heart thumps. Any speech that I imagined delivering flies out of my head, and all I can do is gulp past the lump in my throat.

"To apologize."

"Okay."

"I'm sorry."

"Thank you."

Our words bounce off each other, with barely a breath between them. Then, silence hangs heavy. I swallow again, struggling to find the words to tell her what I feel.

"I was an ass, Margot. I should never have gotten mad at you. I told you it didn't matter who the father was, and then I went back on that."

"I understand. I probably should have told you sooner."

Wringing my hands together, I lick my lips. "I care about you and I care about the baby, Margot. I made a mistake. I want to be here."

"I can see that," she says. Her voice is flat, and alarm bells start ringing in my head. Margot stares at a pile of magazines on the coffee table, and I can see the tension heightening between us. Silence stretches, second by second, until Margot finally drags her gaze back to mine.

"There's something you need to know," she says.

My mind races. What else could there possibly be? Is there another man? Something about Beckett?

My face feels hot as my heart starts to thud. My fingertips tingle, and still, Margot doesn't speak.

She takes a deep breath, putting a hand over her baby bump. "I have Huntington's disease."

I stare at her, blinking. "You have what?"

"Huntington's disease. My mother had it, too."

My eyes flick to her bump, and Margot lets out a sad sigh.

"I'm not sure about the baby."

"What... What's Huntington's?" My mouth is dry. I try to lick my lips to transfer a bit of moisture, but my tongue barely has any to spare. My heart is still thumping. I force myself to sit still and listen.

"It's a brain disorder." Margot extends her hands, and I see a slight shake as she holds them in front of her. "This will get worse. Anxiety and depression are common, which might explain why I've suffered from both."

She smiles sadly at me before shifting her gaze to the

back window. I see her throat bob as she swallows, her hand moving in slow circles around her stomach.

"My mother was irritable and angry for many of our teen years," Margot says. Her eyes are soft, and I know she's far away in her mind. "In the end, she was pretty aggressive and angry. Very different from the soft, loving mother that we grew up with. I wasn't there when she died. I've told myself that it's because I was working to provide for my family, but to be honest, it was because I couldn't face what she'd become."

Margot takes a deep breath, staring down at her bump.

"I can handle the tremors," she says softly. "I'm not afraid of not being able to walk, or to struggle to swallow. I'm ready to lose control over my body. But my mind..."

"Margot." I reach over and put a hand on her thigh, but she flinches away.

A tear rolls down Margot's cheek, and she shakes her head. "It's better this way, Dante. It's better to stop this now. We had fun, and it ended badly between us, but at least it ended before I turn into someone else."

"No." I shake my head. "No."

"It's not your choice." Margot lifts her eyes up to mine, straightening her back. Her gaze hardens, and her teeth clench together. "I don't want you to see me fall apart. I'd rather you remember me as the person I am now, instead of dragging you down with me. It's too much of a burden to put on another person. I won't do that to you."

"You don't get to decide what's best for me, Margot," I answer with a strangled voice. "What if I said I want to be there for you?"

"I'd tell you that you were stupid. You have no idea what you'd be signing up for."

"What about the baby? Doesn't the baby deserve a father?"

"Yes," Margot nods. "But I'm not going to be the one to take your life away from you. I'm not going to force you into throwing your freedom away just to take care of me and my baby. It's not fair, Dante."

"I'm not throwing anything away. I'm here for you."

Margot smiles sadly. She stands up and reaches over to put her hands on either side of my face. I put my palms over her hands, searching her eyes. I look for something—anything—that will tell me she'll change her mind.

"Live your life, Dante. Find someone healthy, happy, and unencumbered. Don't try to be a hero. Trust me, the guilt of holding you back would kill me faster than the disease."

"Margot, you're wrong."

"And you have no idea what you're talking about."

She leans down, pressing her lips to mine. "I love you, Dante. I do. That's why I'm not going to let you be with me."

"Margot..."

"Go back to Argyle."

Margot straightens up, smiling sadly at me. She gives me a soft nod.

I can't move from the armchair where I'm seated. I'm pinned to the cushion, staring up at the woman I love.

She thinks she's doing this for me, but she can't see my heart being ripped out of my chest right in front of her. She can't see the hope being extinguished inside me.

There won't be someone else who's happy, and healthy, and unencumbered. I already know that. The only woman who has made me want to live my life to its fullest has been Margot. In all the years I've been on this earth, she's the only one who's made me want to leave Argyle.

There's no one else. There never will be.

But Margot still walks away. I listen to her footsteps fade

as she makes her way back up to her room. I sit on her sofa, shell-shocked, heartbroken, and alone.

34

MARGOT

I THOUGHT I'd go straight up to my room and cry, but instead, I lay in bed and a feeling of complete calm washes over me.

I'm sad, of course, but I'm strong.

For the first time in my life, I've faced my problems head-on. I told him the truth, and I took the hard path. The right path.

Dante deserves better.

I love him with all my heart, and that's why I need to let him go. Now, he knows why. He can have closure. Even if he says he wants to be there for me, he doesn't understand, and I don't want to be the one to hold him back.

Still, when I lay in bed, I think about seeing him at family events. Ivy is married to Luca, so I'm sure I'll cross paths with him.

What if he gets married to someone else?

Pain slices across my chest and I squeeze my eyes shut until it passes.

It's for the best.

Letting Dante go is the first truly good thing I've ever done. It's the only time I've been strong not only for myself, but for someone else. It's the first step in being the kind of person I want to be. The kind of person I need to be for my child.

I close my eyes, and another wave of pain washes over me. I can sense Prince Dante's presence downstairs, even though I can't hear anything. I can *feel* him in the house, so close to me.

But I can never have him.

Knowing that I told him the truth, and that I broke it off with him for his own sake gives me strength. Any time I feel the urge to tiptoe out of my room and go find him—even for one last kiss—I hold myself back.

I'm strong.

I'm honest.

I'm doing this for him.

When I hear the guest bedroom door close down the hall, a tear escapes my eyes. It soaks into my pillow, and I turn my back to the door.

I made the right choice.

It had to end.

It's the only way.

...Right?

THE NEXT MORNING is cold and grey. When I go downstairs, Dante is already gone. Luca tells me he flew out of the Kingdom at first light, and a sharp pain pierces my chest.

It's for the best.

I know it is. I keep telling myself it is. Last night, I was even proud of myself for breaking it off with him for good.

So, why does it hurt so badly?

I wrap my fingers around a mug of herbal tea, bringing it

up to my lips. Ivy pads into the kitchen, glancing at me. She wrinkles her nose.

"I'd kill for a cup of coffee." She glances over at the coffee machine, her eyebrows arching wistfully.

Squaring my shoulders, I fling my tea into the sink. "Fuck it," I say. "Me, too. The doctor said a coffee once in a while would be fine for the baby. I think we deserve one today. It's nearly Christmas."

Ivy grins, nodding. "I like the way you think."

As soon as the smell of coffee hits my nose, I let out a soft moan. For those few minutes while the coffee is brewing and I drink it, I only think of the pleasure of the hot, bitter liquid on my tongue.

I don't think of Dante or of being alone. I don't think about the fact that he left without saying goodbye, or that I might have to watch him fall in love with someone else.

I just sip my coffee. Bitter, black, liquid gold.

When my mug is empty, though, the Prince floods my mind again. My eyes prickle, and I start to regret pushing him away.

I did this for him.

That's what I need to keep telling myself.

I love him, and that's why I pushed him away. It's best for him if he isn't tied down to me. I can suffer on my own. Raise my child on my own. Stand on my own two feet for once.

If he stayed with me, he'd be signing up for a lifetime of caring for someone sick. He'd be giving his life up for a child that isn't his, and then he'd watch me fall apart in front of him.

Breaking up with him is the kindest thing to do, even if it feels bad.

My baby moves, and I put a hand to my stomach. A few

violent kicks later, and I'm giggling with Ivy as she touches my belly.

That's all it takes for me to snap out of my mood. I spend the rest of the day focused on my baby, planning a renovation in one of the guest bedrooms to turn it into a nursery. Ivy pores over Pinterest boards with me, and not for the first time, I'm grateful to have my sister by my side.

A WEEK LATER, though, on Christmas Day, I'm dealt another blow. Ivy stares at me across the dinner table and announces that she and Luca will be moving out into their own place.

I blink back tears and paint a smile on my face. "I don't know why I'm surprised."

"It's not that we don't love living here," Ivy says. "It's just that we're ready to have our own space. The babies will be here in less than three months, and we'd like to have the house set up before then."

I nod, wrapping my arms around my sister. She hugs me tight, but it does nothing to dispel the emptiness I feel inside.

I'll be alone. Again.

But instead of spiraling into self-doubt and self-pity, I square my shoulders and force myself to smile at my sister. "Do you have a house picked out yet?"

She shakes her head. "We have some viewings set up for the first week of January. Will you come with us?"

I nod, smiling. "Of course."

Ivy's face brightens as she lets out a relieved sigh. "Thanks, Margot. I was worried you'd be mad at me. We've lived together for so long, and I didn't want you to feel like I was abandoning you."

"Not at all," I lie.

I swallow past a lump in my throat, turning my face away

from her as I compose myself. Taking a few calming breaths, I force myself to think of the positives.

From the moment I found out I was pregnant, I feel like things have been happening in quick succession. Within months, my entire life is turning on its head.

But that's not a bad thing.

Even with Dante, as sad as I am to see him go, I'm glad that he was in my life. The few weeks that we spent together gave me hope that I can still have happiness in my life. Even if I never meet anyone like him again, I know that my life isn't doomed.

I have hope for the future, which is something I never would have thought when I got my diagnosis.

Maybe, even with this disease, I can still live a full life with the time that I have left.

35

DANTE

A SHORT, grey-haired woman with perfectly round glasses smiles at me from behind a reception desk when I walk through the door. A few people are sitting down in the waiting area, and the whole room is plastered with informational posters and motivational quotes.

The reception desk has large, block letters proclaiming the organization's name: Huntington's Disease Society of America.

I'm in New York City, at the organization's head office. Just over two weeks ago, Margot told me she didn't want me in her life. I've spent every waking hour researching her disease, and it's landed me in the United States. If I'm going to show Margot that I'm not afraid, I need to prove it to her.

"You must be Prince Dante," the woman behind the desk says, and all heads turn toward me. "Welcome to HDSA! I'm Lou."

"Thank you," I answer, nodding to her and then to the people waiting in the room.

The woman jumps up from her chair with surprising agility, moving from her chair behind the desk to beckon me forward. "Let me show you around. Vicky said you'd be here today."

"Thanks for having me on such short notice."

"Oh, please," Lou says with a grin. "We wouldn't turn down royalty. We just re-opened after the holidays, and we're glad to have you."

Lou chatters the entire time she leads me down a long hallway. She points out different offices for doctors and administrators, gives me a handful of brochures, and tells me about all the work that the organization does for people suffering from Huntington's.

"So, what made you decide to reach out? It was quite a surprising phone call to get, let me tell you! I never thought I'd be on the phone with a Prince!"

I clear my throat, hesitating. "I met someone with Huntington's, and..."

My voice trails off, and Lou just nods. "I get it. Welcome." She smiles at me before knocking on one of the doors, not waiting for an answer before opening it.

"Vicky! The Prince is here." She glances at me, laughing. "Never thought I'd say those words."

"Thanks, Lou. Come in, please." Vicky motions for me to enter, nodding at Lou to close the door behind me. She pulls out a chair for me, then takes a seat beside me.

Her face is kind, with deep-set, dark brown eyes. Her brown hair is streaked with grey, pulled back in a low bun. She's wearing a long scarf around her neck and a simple wedding band on her ring finger.

"Thank you for coming in," she says, smiling.

"It's no problem. I appreciate you taking me in on such short notice."

"You mentioned you wanted to volunteer, and you wanted to see how we run things here?"

I nod. My voice seems to have disappeared, and I clear my throat to try to coax it back. "I have a...friend..."

My eyes mist up, and Vicky puts her hand on my knee. The touch surprises me—people don't usually touch me—but it's remarkably comforting. She doesn't say anything, she just sits there and waits for me to continue.

I take a deep breath. "I have a friend who was diagnosed, and she, uh—" I rough a hand through my hair. Why are words so hard? "She sort of pushed me away after telling me about it. I was hoping that if I came here and learned about the disease, maybe I could show her that... I don't know. That I'm not afraid?"

Vicky lets out a sigh, nodding. "You're very brave."

That makes me laugh, and for the first time in a long time, a tear falls down my cheek. Without skipping a beat, Vicky grabs some tissues from beside her and pulls three of them out, handing them to me.

Wiping my face, then crumpling the tissues in my hand, I lift my eyes up to hers. "So, is there anything I can do to help?"

Vicky grins. "There's lots you can do to help, Your Highness."

EVEN THOUGH EVERYTHING I'm doing is way out of my comfort zone, it feels right. I get a room at a hotel near the center, and I spend every day helping out. Sometimes, all I do is make phone calls to confirm patients' appointments. I tidy the waiting room and make sure things are organized. I listen to Lou nattering and nod politely when she tells me about her grandchildren.

I ask Vicky a thousand questions, and she shows me how

she got the center started, and how it grew into the national organization that it is today.

After a few days, Vicky introduces me to some of the patients. From then on, every day, I get to talk to people who have been affected by the disease. To my surprise, I start gravitating toward the family members and carers that come in with the patients.

I develop a dark sort of sense of humor with the people that I meet, and without even asking me, they understand that I can relate to them.

Every day, I think of Margot. She's on her own in Farcliff, with only a small support system and no organizations like this one to help her out.

My family knows where I am, but they don't know what I'm doing. I refuse Theo's repeated offers to send a security team to me, and I just focus on my day-to-day work. Once again, I become mostly invisible. No one knows me as the Prince of Argyle. No one thinks of me as Beckett's brother. No one knows about my past, or about Margot, or anything else.

I'm just a volunteer at an organization for a debilitating, incurable disease.

I work. I learn. I prepare.

When Margot told me that I was better off finding someone healthy, happy, and unencumbered, I knew it came from a good place. I knew she thought she was doing the right thing by pushing me away.

But it wasn't the right thing.

The place I'm supposed to be is by her side. When she walked away from me, I wanted to scream, but I knew it would be useless.

I turned my back on her once, and I showed her that I wasn't strong enough.

The only way for me to prove to her that I can be by her side—that I *want* to be by her side—is by showing her that I'm not afraid of what the future might bring us. I can only think of one way of doing that, and that means I need to spend some time learning about her diagnosis.

By the time two months pass in New York, my heart aches for Margot. I miss her so much that pain almost feels like part of me, but I still have hope.

I have hope that she'll see that I'm worthy of her. Hope that she'll believe me when I say I'll be by her side. Hope that however many years she's on this earth, she'll want me there with her.

At the end of two months, I feel like I know even less than I knew before, but my eyes are open. With Vicky's help, I take everything I've learned and I go back to Farcliff.

Back to my love.

Back to my future.

Back to Margot.

36

MARGOT

After Ivy moves into her own place, I decide to sell the mansion. What does a single woman need seven bedrooms for?

Even with a nursery, there are still five bedrooms that are going unused.

The only positive about this house is the privacy. It's a fortress, and I feel safe from prying eyes in here.

Safe, and alone.

In the silence, I always miss Dante.

I know, I know. I'm the one who pushed him away—but the heart isn't a simple organ. I pushed him away because it was best for *him*, not necessarily for me. I didn't want to tie him down to a hard, painful life.

As the weeks drag on, though, I start to think that maybe it wasn't selfless.

Wasn't I just protecting myself? By pushing him away, wasn't I making sure that he wouldn't turn his back on me again? That he wouldn't hurt me like he did in Argyle? That I would be alone, but at least it would be on *my* terms?

And on another level, wasn't I just protecting myself from the guilt of subjecting him to the life of a carer?

I saw what this disease did to my family. It tore us apart. Ivy was the only one that was strong enough to stay by Mama's side. Even our father took off the first chance he got. For the past decade, he's been living life bouncing from place to place, not worried about anything except forgetting the past.

I don't want to see that happen to Dante.

The only thing I can do is move forward.

As my due date approaches, a nervous excitement builds inside me. I can't wait to meet my baby. This little bundle of strength that has carried me through so much heartache in the past few months will be here soon, and I will be solely responsible for him.

At least, I think it's a him. I decided not to find out, but it feels like a boy.

IN EARLY MARCH, four weeks before my due date, I walk into my doctor's office and take a seat for a routine appointment. A pamphlet catches my eye from the wall of brochures. Heaving myself off my chair, I waddle over to it.

A new center dedicated to supporting those with Huntington's has opened up in Farcliff. My eyebrows arch, and I read every word on the thin pamphlet three times before the doctor calls my name.

I don't hear much of what the OB-GYN has to say during that appointment. I only know that everything is normal with the baby, and that I know exactly where I'll be headed after my doctor is done talking.

She smiles at me after typing up a few notes on the

computer. "You look much better, Margot. I was worried about you for a while, but you seem a lot stronger."

"I guess I'm a mother, now. I have to be."

The doctor smiles as she stands up, leading me back out to the lobby. I head to the car and slide into the back seat. My driver glances back at me.

"Home?"

"No," I answer, pulling the pamphlet out of my purse. "Here."

He glances at the address, nodding.

My heart races as we drive toward the center. I don't even know why I'm nervous. I've suffered on my own for so long that having other people who might understand what I'm going through seems like too much of a luxury.

Plus, if I show up there, I'll surely be recognized. I haven't told the public about my diagnosis yet, and I'm sure Felicity would want to do it in a professional, official way.

A part of me is sick of hiding, though.

Why should I hide my diagnosis? Why should I live in fear of what the future holds?

If the past couple of months have taught me anything, it's that I'm able to survive on my own. I'm stronger than I thought I was, and I can face my disease instead of hiding away from it.

Still, when we pull up outside a small shopfront with a temporary sign hanging up above it, my heart stutters. I sit there for a few moments, staring.

"Would you like me to come in with you, Miss LeBlanc?" my driver asks.

I shake my head, forcing a smile. "That's all right. Why don't you take the rest of the day off?"

"How will you get home?"

"I'll find a way," I grin. "I can Uber or taxi or call Ivy. It'll be fine. Please. Take the day."

The driver's face splits into a smile. He nods, thanking me before helping me out of the back seat. Every movement is difficult. I've had to get all slip-on shoes now, because I can't even tie my own laces. I take a deep breath, painting a smile on face as I watch him get back into the car and drive away.

Then, I turn to the building's door and push it open.

I don't know what I was expecting, but it isn't this. I'm greeted with a moderate-sized, inviting room. Three couches are set up on one side, with comfortable-looking cushions and throws on them. Baskets of books and magazines are dotted around the place, and soft music is playing over a small speaker. A tabletop water feature is bubbling on a side table, with more books lined up beside it. A half-finished crossword is on the coffee table with a pen lying across it, ready to be completed by the next waiting person.

A woman, probably in her late forties or early fifties, is hanging a picture on a wall. She turns to look at me when I step inside.

Her face breaks into a smile, and her kind, brown eyes soften.

"Hello, there. Welcome to the Huntington's Disease Society of Farcliff." She shakes her head. "News sure does travel fast. We only opened today."

I lift up the pamphlet. "I saw this."

"Oh," she says, smiling as she frowns. "I didn't know those had been distributed yet. Maybe Dante did it."

My heart stops. "I'm sorry, what?"

"Oh, pardon me," she says, tucking a strand of hair behind her ear. "I'm Vicky. I'm the director of the New York chapter of the Society in America, just here to help set up the organization in your Kingdom. We won't be affiliated, but I felt that I could help." She frowns, tilting her head. "You look familiar."

"Margot," I answer, extending a hand.

She shakes it, glancing down at my stomach. "Congratulations."

I nod in thanks, smiling. I clear my throat as my heart starts to thump. "Sorry, you said that someone had distributed the pamphlets? Did you say Dante?"

Vicky's cheeks redden and she waves a hand. "Dave. I said Dave. He's setting up the center here. Lovely young man."

The woman averts her eyes, taking a few steps away from me. "Tea? Coffee?"

"No, thanks. Are you sure you didn't say Dante?"

She gulps, shaking her head. "His name is Dave. He's out at the moment, but he might be back later. He likes to stay in the background, though. Would you like to sit down? I can tell you about the services we offer."

She smiles at me, motioning to one of the couches. I nod, taking a seat, but I can't quite let it go.

Am I just hearing things? I'm sure she said Dante's name.

But she wouldn't. She couldn't.

What would Dante have to do with any of this?

I'm just hung up on him, so I'm hearing his name and seeing his face everywhere. It's not him. It's Dave.

Then, the front door opens and a man steps through, carrying a large box. His hood is flipped up, but something in the way his body moves makes a lump form in my throat.

"Oh, Dant—Dave," Vicky says, glancing at me quickly. "Thank you. Let me help you with that."

Dave grunts. "It's alright, Vicky, I've got it."

As soon as I hear his voice, a gasp escapes my lips. My baby starts kicking violently, and my hand goes to my stomach.

The man turns to look at me, dropping the box of books he'd been carrying. It falls to the ground with a loud thud, staying upright at his feet.

The air stills, and my jaw drops.

Prince Dante stares at me with wide eyes, the vein in his neck pumping furiously. I watch him swallow, pushing his hood back as he smooths his hand through his hair.

"Margot," he rasps. "I didn't think you'd come."

37

DANTE

I SET up this center in the hope that I'd see her here. I put that pamphlet at her doctor's office in the hope that she'd show up. The last two months of my life have been dedicated to Margot.

Still, I wasn't ready.

"Dante," Margot whispers, standing up. The sound of my name on her tongue sends shock waves through my body. Her voice roots me to the ground, making my skin tingle from head to toe. Cold, heavy metal fills my chest, making it hard for me to breathe.

I can't speak. There are no words.

Margot is here, more pregnant and more beautiful than I could ever have expected. She's kept her hair short, and her blue eyes are shining as she takes a step toward me.

She pauses, the width of the room still between us.

It's too far. Too much. I need her in my arms, in my life, in my heart.

Vicky, bless her, clears her throat. "You two, uh, know each other?"

That's enough to snap me out of my stupor. "Yeah. We do," I answer, still staring at Margot. There's a magnet pulling me toward her. A string, connecting my gut to hers, tugging me in her direction.

So, I comply.

I take a step toward the love of my life.

There's only one problem: the box of book donations that I dropped at my feet. Too heavy to kick out of the way, and too big to step over.

I stumble. My upper body pitches forward as my feet stay stuck behind the box. I try to step over it again to catch myself, but it's too tall. I yelp, falling forward and landing in a heap on the floor.

I spend two months working to build this center for Margot, and this is how I present it to her? The best way I have to convince her to be with me is to fall flat on my face the moment I see her?

My face burns. I push myself off the floor with my hands, moving my legs around the box to find my footing.

Then, I feel it.

A hand.

No, not just any hand on my back. *Her* hand.

Just a couple of layers of fabric away from touching my skin.

Angling my face upward, I see Margot standing before me. Her eyes are soft, her lips parted, her brows drawing together.

"Are you okay?"

Is there anything sweeter than the sound of Margot LeBlanc's voice? The way it dances on her tongue? The way her mouth moves to shape the letters?

I stand up, now only inches from her. Nodding, I clear my throat. "I'm fine. You?"

"I'm good. Ready to get this kid out of me."

Margot's smile is like a balm on my aching heart.

"April 1st, right? That's coming up soon."

Margot nods. "Not soon enough. I can't even tie my own shoes anymore."

A lump lodges itself in my throat, and a weight takes residence on my chest. Breathing becomes difficult, but I force myself to suck in as much air as I need to speak.

"What do you think?" I croak, sweeping an arm around at the small waiting room.

Margot's eyes follow the movement, and I take the opportunity to drink her in. She's gained a little bit of weight, and her face has lost its sharp angles. Now, it's all soft, feminine curves. Her cheekbones are still defined, but they're no longer razor-sharp. Her lips are full. Her eyes, bright.

She puts a hand to her lower back, letting her eyes drift all around the room. Finally, she brings them back to me, smiling. "I like it."

"Did Vicky tell you what services we offer? I think we'll be able to help lots of people not just with education but with counseling and support. We're thinking of setting up a fundraising branch dedicated to research, too."

"We?" Her eyebrows jump up. "You work here?"

Vicky laughs softly beside us, and both Margot and I turn to look at her. The older woman looks at Margot kindly, shaking her head. "Honey, he's the beating heart of this place. It was his idea, from conception to execution. He's a magician on the computers, and he even helped us back in New York to update our systems. He doesn't work here. He *created* it."

I swallow thickly. I don't have the courage to look at Margot to see her reaction, so I just stare at Vicky.

Vicky, ever sharp, tilts her head as she looks at Margot. "He told me he had a friend who pushed him away after opening up about her diagnosis. If I were a betting woman, I'd say that friend was you. I'd also say that 'friend' isn't exactly accurate."

I can hear Margot's breath speed up. I can sense every tiny movement that she makes, even though I'm not looking at her.

Touching her hair, cradling her bump, even blinking faster as she takes in Vicky's words.

Finally, I force myself to look at her.

"You did this for me?" Margot whispers.

My heart races. How is it possible to love one woman this much? It makes everything difficult, even answering a simple question.

I nod, struggling to force the word out. "Yeah."

"Why?"

"To show you that I wasn't afraid."

Margot's bottom lip trembles and her eyes fill with tears.

She's only inches away from me, but the distance is still too much. I clear my throat to try to dislodge the boulder that seems to have taken up residence inside it. "Is it too much?"

Then, Margot laughs.

Not a polite laugh. Not a guarded laugh.

A real, genuine laugh.

Open-mouthed, eyes shining, stomach heaving, big, *real* belly-laugh.

She shakes her head. "It's not too much. No one has ever done anything like this for me before." Taking a step toward me, Margot puts her hand to my cheek. "This is..."

Margot's voice trails off as her eyes shine. I put my palm over hers, gulping as I try to find the words to tell her how I feel.

"Margot, I'm not afraid of your illness. I've learned as

much as I can learn in the past couple of months, and I'll continue to learn. Ask Vicky how much work I've done!" I inhale, curling my fingers around her hand. "I want to show you that I can do it. I can be by your side and support you. I won't be giving up my life for you. I'll be *gaining* my life back. I have nothing without you."

She's trembling. The love of my life puts a hand to her baby bump, taking a shaky breath as she closes her eyes. A tear rolls down her cheek.

"Dante..."

"No. Margot, listen to me. Look at me." I wait until she opens her eyes. I cup her cheeks, hoping that I can make her understand the strength of my emotion. "I *love* you, Margot. I know you think that I'd be sacrificing too much by being with you, but I'm sacrificing more by being without you. Let me be by your side. Let me love you the way you deserve to be loved. Let me choose you."

Margot's bottom lip trembles as she inhales. She stares at me, her brows arching. I can feel the tension inside her ratcheting up, and I stroke her cheeks with my thumbs.

"Margot," I whisper. "Let me love you."

"I'm scared." Her voice is a breath. A whisper.

"Of what?"

"That you'll hate me. That you'll regret it." Margot sucks her bottom lip between her teeth before letting out a sigh. "That you'll leave."

My heart breaks all over again when I see how much I've hurt her. When I pushed her away after finding out about Beckett, I drove a wedge between us that seems almost impossible to overcome. I showed her that I wasn't strong enough to handle what life would throw at us. I told her that *she* wasn't enough.

I let out a breath, leaning my forehead against hers.

"I won't."

Those two words don't seem like enough, but how many words would be? What else can I say, except the truth?

I won't hate her. Never. How could I?

I won't regret it. The only regret I have is pushing Margot away.

I won't leave. Never, ever, ever. Not in a million years. Not even if she pushes me away for the next decade. For the next century. I'm here. Always.

Margot puts her hands against my chest, pulling her head away from mine to look into my eyes. I meet her gaze, staring into the eyes of the woman I adore.

"I love you, Margot," I say. "I'm not going anywhere."

Another tear slides down her cheek, but Margot smiles. Her lips stretch, her eyes shine, and her hands curl into my shirt.

I watch Margot's throat bob as she swallows.

Finally, she speaks. "Okay."

That one word saves me.

It's not poetic. It's not eternal prose. It's not a lengthy profession of love...

...but it's perfect.

Okay means yes. It means she'll let me in. It means all this hasn't been for nothing.

Okay means *I love you, too.*

My heart flips in my chest as a laugh bubbles up through me. "Okay?"

She nods, smiling through her tears. "Okay."

Pulling me toward her by my shirt, Margot kisses me, and my world is complete. The instant her lips touch mine, I know I'm the luckiest man in the world.

Her kiss is magic. It's healing, it's hopeful, it's her heart, and it's all mine. Wrapping my arms around the woman of my dreams, I tangle my fingers into her short hair and kiss her harder. Our tongues dance, our breaths mix, and our hearts beat as one.

When I drop to my knees and press my lips to her belly, tears start sliding down my cheeks.

"Hi there," I say to the baby, putting my hands on her stomach. "I'm your father."

A tiny, strangled sob escapes Margot, and she places her hand on my head. I rest my cheek against her stomach, breathing in her scent, her aura, her love.

Then, the baby kicks me right in the jaw. I jump back, yelping, and Margot laughs. She lifts her shirt up, and I see tiny feet pushing out from inside her. My eyes widen as I stare, on my knees in front of her.

"He does that when he's happy," Margot explains. "He must like the idea of having you as a dad."

"He?"

Margot shrugs, smiling. "I decided not to find out, but I think it's a boy. He's always kicking and moving around."

I let out a long sigh, putting my hand against my son's foot. He kicks against me a few more times before settling down, and another lump forms in my throat.

Vicky lets out a sigh, and we both turn to see her wiping her eyes with a tissue. I'd forgotten she was there. She shakes her head at us, turning away. "It's too much. Too perfect. My poor heart can't take this. I need to go call my kids."

Blowing her nose into the tissue, she turns and shuffles down the hallway toward the office.

Margot laughs, her hands still tangled in my hair as I kneel in front of her.

I look up, my heart overflowing with happiness. I can't stop smiling. There's a tingling sensation through my whole body, and my chest feels light.

I hold the love of my life in my arms, knowing I'll never let her go.

EPILOGUE

MARGOT

Turns out, I was wrong. We didn't have a boy after all.

Our baby girl, Hope, was born at 2:36pm on the first of April, after a thirteen-hour labor. She weighed a whopping nine pounds, four ounces. I guess she was enjoying her existence inside me, and didn't want to come out at all. She entered this world kicking and screaming, like the fighter she is.

When Dante held her for the first time, he melted into a puddle of fatherly goo on the hospital room floor. I cried, then. Really cried. Maybe it was the hormones of pregnancy and labor. Maybe it was the emotion of seeing my daughter for the first time.

Whatever it was, I let go of all the nasty feelings that held me back from believing Dante when he said he'd be by my side. I cried, cleansing myself of the past and readying myself for the future with my baby and my soon-to-be husband.

We were married a year later, when my body was mostly recovered and Dante and I had slipped into a happy life together. Our wedding was in Argyle, in the same place that Ivy married Luca. Ivy was my maid of honor, and she cried during the entire ceremony. Having my sister by my side at my wedding meant the world to me. If I'm completely honest, I cried most of the time, too.

Hope and Ivy's twins, Coco and Hazel, acted as flower girls. The three of them were perfect, running down the aisle on clumsy, chubby, one-year-old legs. The three girls were best friends the instant they met when they were a few days old, and they giggled through the wedding, reminding us how much we loved them.

The royal family of Farcliff attended the wedding, but I invited very few celebrities and socialites. It was an intimate affair, but we did release a few pictures to the public afterward.

Shortly after the wedding, I retired from public life. Dante and I moved to a small cottage in the Farcliff countryside, away from prying eyes and overzealous photographers.

It was the peace and quiet we needed to recover from the chaos that our life had been. In that cottage, Dante and I got to know each other again. We made love often, as much as possible, and laughed every chance we got.

We acquired three dogs and a cat. The cat was a stray that followed Dante home one day, and the dogs came from a rescue in Farcliff run by Queen Elle's adoptive father. All four animals adored Hope from the instant they met her.

Ivy and Luca came to see us about once a month to escape the hectic running of *Spoonful of Sugar.*

Hunter and Beckett were both imprisoned for life. I never visited either of them, and after my baby was born, I didn't give them much thought. Neither men deserved my attention, and I was happy to leave them in my past.

. . .

On our two-year anniversary, Dante and I dropped Hope off with her cousins, and Dante took me on a trip to Argyle. King Theo reserved one of the royal islands for us, and we finally had a long-awaited honeymoon weekend.

I'm not ashamed to say I missed Hope so much that I cried on the entire plane ride. In three years, a weekend vacation would be the longest I'd spent away from my daughter.

What can I say? I'm a mother.

Once I saw the clear blue waters and the palm trees, and once I felt the feather pillows and the impossibly comfortable bed, though, my mood changed.

The first night, we just slept.

When we woke up, Dante and I made love to the sounds of the ocean waves lapping the shore. I came in his arms, and I knew there was no one luckier than me.

When we lay tangled in the bedsheets, Dante stroked my face and let out a sigh. "I want another kid," he told me, smiling hopefully.

My chest tightened, and I gulped down my anxieties. "Dante..."

"I know," he interrupted. "It's too much of a risk with the Huntington's gene."

I nodded, unable to answer. We still didn't know if Hope had the disease—we had to wait until she turned eighteen and got the genetic testing done for herself. It was a fifty-fifty chance, and I just couldn't bear the thought of risking it with another child.

"What about adoption?" Dante asked, trailing his fingers over my skin.

My eyes widened, and my heart exploded. I kissed Dante, then, and my love for him multiplied. This man had such a big heart that not only did he take Hope on as his own child, but he wanted more kids to love, even if they weren't his own.

He also took me, flaws and all, and made it his life's purpose to love me just as I loved him.

So, we adopted three more children over the course of the next five years. Our little cottage in the woods soon ran out of space, and we finally moved back to the city to be closer to Ivy and Luca. By that time, media attention around me and Dante had died down to nothing, and we were able to live a normal life.

The Huntington's Disease Society of Farcliff grew to support hundreds of people living with the disease as well as their carers. Dante was a champion of the cause, reminding me every day with his dedication to the HDSF that he was doing this for me.

I never doubted him again. For the rest of our days, Dante never faltered. He was never afraid as my illness progressed, and never fearful of the future. He was by my side, always.

Even when my tremors got worse. Even when I had trouble walking. Even when my mood swings became more extreme, and I started truly fearing the end.

He was there beside me, loving me fully and unconditionally.

Now, eighteen years after Hope's birth, she sits across from Dante and me with an envelope in her hands. My daughter takes a shaking breath, dragging her eyes up to mine.

"I'm scared."

"I know, honey," I say, leaning against Dante. "You can do it. Trust me, it's better to know for sure."

When Hope rips the envelope open, my heart falters. If I passed on the disease to my daughter, I know it will be the killing blow. I won't have the energy to fight much longer if I know I've condemned my daughter to an early grave.

But Hope lets out a relieved breath, lifting her eyes up to mine. "Negative."

Tears slide down my cheeks as my daughter throws her arms around me and Dante. The three of us cry happy tears, and I know that we named our daughter appropriately.

She's always been the Hope in our lives.

She gave me hope before she was born, when I was on my own and life was bleak. She gave Dante the courage to come back to me, hopeful that we'd end up together.

Our daughter is the beacon of hope that will carry on long after Dante and I are gone.

Then, our three other teenagers come barreling through the door, home from their day at school. They descend on the kitchen and eat everything in sight like a pack of hungry wolves. In just a few minutes, the fridge is picked clean. All three of them give me a kiss and ask me when dinner will be ready.

Just like that, life is back to normal.

Dante puts his arm around me, kissing the top of my head. His love for me permeates everything, and I know that I would never have been this happy if we hadn't found each other. He's braver, stronger, and more loving than I could ever hope for in a partner.

He's my Dante. My love. My husband. My life.

All four of our kids are healthy. My husband is beside me. I can rest easy, now, knowing that they'll take care of each other even after I'm gone.

EXTENDED EPILOGUE

DANTE

In Argyle, my birthday was usually full of warm winter sun, sand, and maybe a bit of surfing. Growing up, I'd try to hide away from my family, but they always found me tucked away in some corner of the castle and drag me out to celebrate.

In Farcliff, my birthday is full of snow.

I wake up early to a fresh, white blanket over the world. It takes me thirty minutes to clear the driveway enough to get the car out. I run inside to give Margot one last kiss.

"I'll be back in an hour and a half, I just need to sign some paperwork at the center."

"Okay," Margot mumbles, turning around in bed. "Where are the kids?"

Hope is almost seven years old now, and her little brother, Ollie, is two. We adopted Ollie when he was a baby, and he brought another wave of joy—and sleepless nights—into our lives.

"They're still asleep."

"I'll get up now," Margot says, sighing.

"Take your time." I drop another kiss on her forehead. "I'll check on them."

With the kids still asleep and Margot shuffling around the coffee machine, I make my way to the car. After a forty-minute drive to Farcliff, I park the car behind the Huntington's Disease Society Center. Our receptionist is already there. She gives me a broad smile, sliding a stack of paperwork toward me.

"Just need your signature, Your Highness."

"Call me Dante, please. How many times do I have to say it?" I shake my head, smiling. "I'm not much of a Prince anymore."

"You seem like a prince to me," she says, shrugging.

Signing the papers, I duck into the office and make sure I don't have any messages. The center is quiet today, with no planned activities until next week.

Happy that everything is under control, I drive back through the snowy streets toward our cabin outside of town. As soon as I leave the city, I let out a breath.

The snow muffles the sounds, making the air feel heavy and crisp. I drive slowly, cracking my window slightly to feel the fresh air coming in.

After a few years here, I'm finally starting to get used to the cold. A part of me actually likes it.

The best part about cold weather, though, is walking inside a warm house.

When I enter our home, I'm greeted by the clattering paws of our dog, Fletch, on the hardwood floors and a squeal from Hope.

"Happy birthday!" she exclaims, rushing around the corner after Fletch. She's wearing a party hat and a broad grin, throwing her arms around my waist. "Come to the kitchen."

One of Hope's front teeth fell out last week, and she smiles wider, tucking her tongue into the gap. I slip my palm into my daughter's, giving my dog a head rub with my free hand.

In the kitchen, Margot is waiting for us. Ollie's wrapped around her legs, laughing at something only a two-year-old understands. A massive cake sits on the kitchen island with a blaze of candles burning on top of it.

"I had to go to two stores to get enough candles," Margot grins. "You're getting old."

"I must be," I laugh, shielding my face from the heat of the candles.

"Make a wish!" Hope jumps from one foot to the other, her eyes shining as she looks at me. "Blow them out."

I squeeze my eyes shut, thinking of something to wish for.

When I open my eyes again to see my wife, my son, and my daughter staring back at me, I'm not quite sure what else I could want.

More of the same, maybe. More kids. More dogs. More love and laughter.

Taking a deep breath, I blow out all but two candles. I extinguish them with another breath. Hope laughs, clapping her hands. Margot gets to work taking the candles out of the cake, and I grab some plates from the cupboard.

Ollie somehow climbs up onto a chair when both our backs are turned. He smashes his fist into the double chocolate cake, spreading icing and crumbs all over the counter and himself. Margot yelps, grabbing him and whisking him toward the sink, but not before he manages to stuff his face with cake. It's all over his mouth and arm, with a big swipe of chocolate icing across his shirt.

"Yummy," he says, grinning until Margot can't help but laugh.

"Cake for breakfast only happens on birthdays," I say to

Hope, nudging her with my shoulder. "So don't get used to this."

"I know, I know," Hope says, rolling her eyes. "And my birthday isn't until April."

Margot throws me a glance, smiling. Hope will be seven years old in April, and she's already as sassy as a teenager.

The four of us sit around the kitchen island and eat a slice of cake each. Ollie asks for more, but Margot moves quickly, covering the cake up before he can do any damage.

When the kids run off to play, Margot walks up beside me and wraps her arms around my waist.

"What did you wish for?"

"If I tell you, it won't come true."

"Well, I have some presents for you, but first..." Margot reaches into one of our drawers and pulls out a letter. Her eyes shine as she stares at me, a soft smile stretching her lips. "It's the approval letter from the adoption agency. We can have another kid."

"Really?" My eyes widen as I scan the letter. I let out a breath. "That was way quicker than last time."

"If you still want to adopt another one." Margot sucks her lip between her teeth, arching her eyebrows. "You do still want to, right?"

Her voice is small. She stares at me, wide-eyed, as I try to process the information.

We were approved. We can adopt again.

My birthday wish just came true—more kids. More love. More laughter.

"Dante?" Margot asks in a whisper.

Then, I start laughing. I throw my arms around my wife and spin her in a circle in the kitchen, planting a kiss on her lips.

When I set her down again, her eyes are shining. "I'm assuming that's a yes?"

"Of course it's a yes," I say, nuzzling my nose against hers. "That's the best birthday present I could ever ask for."

As soon as I finish the sentence, a loud crash sounds from the next room, followed by the sound of Ollie wailing.

"It's nothing! Don't come in!" Hope calls out.

Margot's shoulders drop as she lets out a sigh. "You're absolutely sure you want another one?"

I chuckle, following her toward the sound of the chaos in the next room.

"I am if you are."

THE REST of my birthday is spent with my family. The kids give me homemade cards, and Margot presents me with a top-of-the-line computer that I've been looking at for months. When the kids fall asleep that evening, Margot and I curl up on the couch. She lays her head in the crook between my shoulder and my chest, and I stroke her hair with the tips of my fingers.

"Thank you for a great day," I tell her.

She smiles, glancing up at my face. "I set up a meeting with the adoption agency for next week, so this might be one of our last times with only two kids."

My heart thumps as my throat tightens. I shake my head, intertwining my fingers with hers. "I love you, Margot."

Pressing her lips to mine, Margot promises me one last birthday present. She takes me by the hand and leads me to the bedroom, locking the door behind us.

When she takes her clothes off, one garment at a time, I know there's no one luckier than me.

I don't need a royal title. I don't need a private island in Argyle. I don't need money or clout.

I just need Margot, the kids, and the life we've built together.

On days like today, Margot and I don't even mention her illness. We don't talk about the future, except to talk about hope and happiness.

When I run my fingers over Margot's body, my heart fills up to the brim. I kiss the woman of my dreams, claiming her lips and tangling my fingers into her hair.

We fall into bed together. I make love to my wife the way she deserves to be loved. I watch the ecstasy pour out of every pore, and I drink up her desire until we're both spent and sleepy, tangled in each other's arms.

With a sigh, Margot rests her cheek against my shoulder. "I love you, Dante."

I hear those four, simple words almost every day, but they never cease to make my heart beat harder. I wrap my arms around my wife and hold her tight.

Sometimes, I forget that she's ill. I live in hope that research for Huntington's disease will progress enough to find a cure before it's too late. I live in the present, trying to soak up every minute we have together.

When she told me she wanted to adopt again, Margot showed me that she feels the same way. We may not have as much time together as a normal, healthy couple, but we're going to make the most of it.

We'll create the family that we want. We'll love our children fiercely and completely, and we'll always be by each other's side.

Margot is everything to me, and when she whispers one last 'happy birthday,' I press a kiss to her temple and hold her close.

Soon, we'll have another child to take care of and even more chaos in our busy household.

But we'll be together, and for me, that's all that matters.

LILIAN
MONROE
WRONG
PRINCE
ROYALLY UNEXPECTED: BOOK SIX

WRONG PRINCE

ROYALLY UNEXPECTED: BOOK 6

1

CARA

ONE DIFFERENCE between regular people and royalty is that regular people knock before entering your home.

Royals, on the other hand?

Knocking isn't part of their vocabulary.

The only warning I get that Prince Theo is at my house is the sound of a vehicle pulling up outside and the driver cutting the engine.

I assume it's one of my parents' friends or maybe a member of our household staff, and I ignore it.

The Crown Prince of Argyle bursts through the door in a blaze of abs and windswept hair, tearing the sunglasses off his bronzed face as he scans the room. A soft breeze follows after him, fluttering the edges of his linen shirt.

"Cara!" he calls out. I stand up, putting my book down on the sofa beside me. He flashes me a brilliant smile. "Come on. We're going."

Every word Theo speaks is a command. He was born a king, and a part of me likes when he speaks like that. There's something attractive about confidence and power, even though I'd never be caught dead saying that out loud.

I'm more of the 'don't tell me what to do' kind of gal—or at least that's what I tell myself. The fluttering in my belly begs to differ.

I frown. "Go where?"

The Prince's white linen shirt is unbuttoned, revealing his chiseled chest. He's wearing teal swimming trunks and a pair of white leather boat shoes. He nods toward the open door, grinning.

"It's the summer solstice. We have a tradition to uphold."

My heart thumps uncomfortably. I thought our traditions had died when Prince Luca's accident happened. That day, everything changed.

Three years ago, my betrothed, Prince Luca—Prince Theo's little brother—jumped off a cliff into shallow water and broke his back. Luca has been trying to recover from his injuries in Singapore, undergoing countless operations and hours of physical therapy.

And me?

I've been shut out. Languishing on the other side of the world. Begging him to talk to me, and then slowly accepting that it's over between us.

At first, I wanted to be there with him. The first year was hell. I called, and called, and called. I cried. I sent letters and messages. I sent him care packages and made sure to try to speak to him every day.

We have a special Post Office box, where we've been exchanging messages since we were kids. I checked it every day for a year, hoping he'd have sent me some note, some parcel, some sign that he cared.

Every day, it was empty.

Luca pushed me away. Slowly but surely, he stopped answering. The rest of the royal family backed away from me as my engagement to Luca fizzled. I didn't just lose my fiancé, I lost all my closest childhood friends.

Luca, Theo, Beckett, Dante—all four brothers became strangers to me. It nearly killed me.

I even went to Singapore a year after the accident, but Luca refused to see me.

The second year, I was in a daze. I don't remember much, except sleeping a lot and not eating much. The past three years have been the loneliest of my life.

It's only in the past six months that I've started coming around again. Slowly, I'm starting to feel like myself again. I'm making plans for the future. Plans for myself.

But Theo's standing here in front of me as if nothing at all has changed.

It *has* changed, though. Being pushed away by Luca is what finally made me decide to leave this Kingdom. I have to. It's the only way I can move on from all this.

Next week, I'm flying to the United States to pursue my dream of becoming a singer. I've applied to two dozen colleges for voice programs and haven't heard back from any of them, but that won't stop me. I'm done with letting people push me away and beat me down. I'm stronger than that. I've stared into the abyss, and now, I'm walking away.

I'll go to Los Angeles and work in a restaurant while I try to make it as a singer. I'll plead with record executives. I'll sing in dirty dive bars. I'll do whatever it takes, even if my parents think singing is beneath our family name.

I need to go. Do something for myself. Pursue a dream I've had since I was a little girl—a dream that predates Luca, and Theo, and all the heartache that the royal family brought me.

Knowing that I'm leaving is the only thing that has kept me going.

Up until two minutes ago, I thought I'd never see the Princes of Argyle again. I thought all four brothers had turned their backs on me after Luca's accident.

Apparently, I was wrong.

I clear my throat, combing my fingers through the ends of my long, brown hair. "Your Highness—"

"Cara," Theo huffs, shaking his head. "Come on. Stop standing there like we didn't spend every moment of our childhood together. Get your bathing suit on and get in my car. We're sailing around the islands."

Argyle is a Caribbean kingdom, complete with white, sandy beaches and waving palm trees. The Kingdom consists of about seventy islands, ranging from land masses the size of Cuba to small atolls with nothing but a single palm tree on them.

Nearly every year since I was seven years old, I've sailed around the Kingdom with the four Princes of Argyle. It takes just over two days to do it, and it's been a highlight of my year, every year, since I was a little girl.

Three years ago, our tradition abruptly stopped. Luca had just had his accident, and we didn't know whether he would recover. Sailing around the islands didn't seem right.

Our yearly sailing trip was yet another thing I mourned.

Prince Theo, the eldest of the Princes of Argyle, stares at me, eyebrows raised. "Well?"

"I thought..." I clear my throat. "I didn't think we were doing that anymore."

"Look, Luca might be refusing to talk to you, but it doesn't mean we aren't friends. We've done this every year since we were kids. It's tradition."

"Dante and Beckett?" I raise my eyebrows, wondering if his two other brothers will come.

Theo shakes his head. "You know how Dante is. Won't

even come out of his office to see the sun. He's developing a new security plan for the palace, and he says he's too busy researching. Beckett is away for the month on a trip across Europe."

"You want to do it without them and Luca?"

"It's the solstice," Theo says, as if that explains anything. "I'm sick of tiptoeing around the castle. Ever since Luca's accident, all of Argyle has been in mourning." He snorts, shaking his head. "No one died! Luca is fine. His physical therapy is going well, even if he refuses to talk to us. The doctors think he'll walk again."

I arch my eyebrows. Luca walking again? That would be nothing short of a miracle. If he recovered, would he want to pick up where we left off?

Would *I* want that?

The churning in my gut tells me no, I wouldn't. I'm leaving Argyle next week. I'm doing something for *me*. I'm pursuing my dreams, not falling back into the arms of a man who didn't want me. Maybe he never wanted me.

It's over between Luca and me. Has been for a long, long time. His recovery won't change that.

"Come on, Cara," Theo continues, taking a step toward me. "I'm sick of it. I need to do something fun. Something normal." He takes a deep breath, spreading his palms toward me. When Theo's sharp, blue eyes land on mine, he arches his eyebrows. "I want to hang out with someone I've been friends with for years. Like old times."

"It's not like old times, though, Theo," I say softly.

Something flashes in Theo's eyes. He's always been the quiet one. The dutiful one. But there's a fierceness in his gaze that makes me pause.

He snorts, shaking his head. "What, because Luca had an accident and decided to turn his back on you? On all of us?"

Theo scoffs. "We've been trying to reach out to him ever since he left for Singapore, Cara. *Three. Years.* He thinks he's being some kind of saint for suffering alone, but he doesn't realize how much it hurts for the rest of us. I've seen how much you've been hurting. He's my brother, but he has no right to treat you like that."

The truth in his words makes my eyes prickle with tears. No one has acknowledged how much pain Luca has caused me. My mother tells me I should just try harder to get Luca to come back to me. My father mostly just avoids talking about it.

I know what my parents' unsaid words mean, though: my betrothal fell apart, and it's all my fault.

My mother won't get her 'in' to the royal family. My father's sponsorships and business will continue to falter. Our family will slowly slip out of Argyle's elite, and I have only myself to blame. I didn't do my duty. I couldn't close the deal.

I failed.

So, I'm leaving.

For once in my life, I'm *not* going to do what's expected of me. I'll leave my home and chase my dream. I'll sing every day and pursue something I never thought I'd have. I'll look for adventure. I'll seek out the unknown. I'll have experiences I could never have imagined.

But when Theo stares at me with those crushed velvet eyes, I hesitate.

Our solstice sailing trip is tradition. It wouldn't hurt to do it one last time, would it?

For old time's sake.

I didn't think anyone understood how heartbreaking it's been to watch Luca turn his back on me and be completely powerless to do anything about it.

Theo understands. I can tell by the way he's looking at me

right now. His eyes are asking me to come with him. To sail around the islands and pretend that none of it ever happened.

And one last time, that's exactly what I'll do. This sailing trip will be my final goodbye. My last look at the islands of my home before I leave on my first big adventure.

I try to gulp past a lump in my throat and finally nod. "Okay."

Theo's face breaks into a blinding smile. He crosses the room in three strides and wraps his arms around me, spinning me in a circle. I yelp, clinging onto his broad shoulders. He smells like salty sea air and a fresh summer breeze. His skin is warm under my touch, and it sends a tingle of energy coursing through my hands. When he sets me down, my cheeks are burning.

Prince Theo is the heir to the throne, and although we grew up together, I'm not used to touching him. I was always promised to Luca, and the other brothers kept a respectful distance.

Theo doesn't seem to notice. He slides his sunglasses on and arches his eyebrows. "Ready?"

"Let me get my swimsuit," I say. "Meet you in the car." Excitement curls in the pit of my stomach as a grin tugs at my lips. I slip away from him, rushing up the stairs in my parents' expansive home. Tearing down the hallway, I run to my bedroom. I take a bag out of my closet and start throwing things in it. A spare swimsuit, a change of clothes, a toothbrush, sunscreen—all the things I'll need for a two-night stay on a royal sailboat.

On top of my dresser, my mismatched collection of shells and beach treasures is proudly displayed. I touch each item for good luck. Wrapping my fingers around an old, faded deck of cards with frayed edges, I smile. Then, I slip it into my bag. My heart flutters, and I fly down the stairs again.

The Prince is already waiting in the car outside, but instead of rushing through the front door, I make a hard left and move deeper into the house toward the library.

Rapping my knuckles gently on the doorframe, I wait for my father's deep voice to call out.

"Come in," he says, and I step through the door.

ALSO BY LILIAN MONROE

For all books, visit:

www.lilianmonroe.com

Brother's Best Friend Romance

Shouldn't Want You

Can't Have You

Don't Need You

Won't Miss You

Military Romance

His Vow

His Oath

His Word

The Complete Protector Series

Enemies to Lovers Romance

Hate at First Sight

Loathe at First Sight

Despise at First Sight

The Complete Love/Hate Series

Secret Baby/Accidental Pregnancy Romance:

Knocked Up by the CEO

Knocked Up by the Single Dad

Knocked Up...Again!

Knocked Up by the Billionaire's Son

The Complete Unexpected Series

Yours for Christmas

Bad Prince

Heartless Prince

Cruel Prince

Broken Prince

Wicked Prince

Wrong Prince

Fake Engagement/ Fake Marriage Romance:

Engaged to Mr. Right

Engaged to Mr. Wrong

Engaged to Mr. Perfect

Mr Right: The Complete Fake Engagement Series

Mountain Man Romance:

Lie to Me

Swear to Me

Run to Me

The Complete Clarke Brothers Series

Extra-Steamy Rock Star Romance:

Garrett

Maddox

Carter

The Complete Rock Hard Series

Sexy Doctors:

Doctor O

Doctor D

Doctor L

The Complete Doctor's Orders Series

Time Travel Romance:

The Cause

A little something different:

Second Chance: A Rockstar Romance in North Korea

Made in the USA
Coppell, TX
02 November 2020

40635251R00166